6/03

DEEP

DEEP

SUSANNA VANCE

DELACORTE PRESS

Published by
Delacorte Press
an imprint of
Random House Children's Books
a division of Random House, Inc.
New York

The trademark Delacorte Press® is registered in the U.S. Patent and
Trademark Office and in other countries.

Visit us on the Web! www.randomhouse.com/teens
Educators and librarians, for a variety of teaching tools,
visit us at www.randomhouse.com/teachers

Library of Congress Cataloging-in-Publication Data
        Deep / Susanna Vance.
            p. cm.
Summary: Somewhere in the Caribbean, seventeen-year-old Morgan and thirteen-year-old Birdie, two girls whose
lives are worlds apart, are brought together.
        ISBN 0-385-73057-8 (trade)—ISBN 0-385-90080-5 (lib. binding)
        [1. Interpersonal relations—Fiction.   2. Seafaring life—Fiction.   3. Kidnapping—Fiction.   4. Caribbean
Area—Fiction.]   I. Title.
        PZ7.V2767 De 2003
        [Fic]—dc21

                                                                            2002012502

The text of this book is set in 13-point Minion Condensed.

Book design by Marci Senders

Printed in the United States of America

May 2003

10 9 8 7 6 5 4 3 2 1

BVG

To my granddaughters,
Alex Lacey Sherburne Stanton,
Amy Elizabeth Mitchell,
Lily Jac Sherburne,
whose passionate hearts and glittering minds
deepen my days,
lighten my nights

ACKNOWLEDGMENTS

Special thanks to my mother, Myla Dorothy Jean Blake Vance, who believes in fairies, and in me.

Thanks to my agent, Robin Rue, who radiates charm, grandeur, and success throughout the kingdom of New York. To creative Emily Kim and to Writers House, who so elegantly look their parts.

Thanks to my editor, Wendy Loggia, who listens to my characters as though they were her children, feeds them brilliant tidbits, and sends them out to play. To Beverly Horowitz and the gracious staff at Random House.

Great appreciation to Literary Arts for bestowing upon me the 2001 Literary Fellowship, Edna Holmes Literary Fund. This fellowship, along with a generous award of residency at the Caldera wilderness facility for writers and artists, contributed significantly toward the completion of *Deep*.

Thank you, one and all.

There they sat, both grown up
and yet children—children in heart;
and it was summer ...

from *The Snow Queen,*
Hans Christian Andersen

One Girl

This is what they'll say on my book jacket: "Brilliant thirteen-year-old perfects both the cartwheel and the metaphor!" They'll say, "America's youngest bestselling authoress is *deep*. Her words come in parrot-bright colors and fly straight into your heart."

They'll mention that my talents come from hardship: that I live where it rains constantly and you can never get tan. That my parents spend too much time thinking about me. That I had asthma when I was little, and got a plain PC for my birthday instead of an orange Mac.

I've been through *a lot* and it's made me deep.

I live in Oregon, I'm an only child, and I'm awesome.

You probably know me: My name is Birdie Sidwell.

Another Girl

I believe myself to be seventeen years of age, the number of marks carved inside the teakwood belly of my sailboat, just above the radar-tracking screen. My name is there, and then seventeen marks. My family did not celebrate birthdays, although I believe others from Norway do. The shortest day of each year, my father would add my mark. Oona, my older sister, had only gotten twelve. The baby boy, none at all; no name, no marks.

My parents forgot to add my last mark, so I carved it myself. Rum brings forgetfulness, and mistakes. I've left my parents behind because mistakes cannot be made at sea. Ask Oona. I still do, although she is far below now, somewhere in the deep.

I live at sea, I am alone, and I am awestruck.

You do not know me: My name is Morgan Bera.

chapter

Birdie

ere I am again, floating in a warm bubble bath, hoping for something heinous or preposterous or even gruesome to happen. I need that, to write my book. If it weren't for the number one rule, "Write about what you know," I'd have written my book already.

Each time I sink to the bottom of the tub, my eyes bulge, my hair billows like scarlet seaweed, and new ideas burst in my head. Like colorful bubbles—like jets of brilliance—like hatchling wordpearls! My brain's like one of those magic crystals you drop in water and it turns into something fabulous.

If I wanted to write a book about thirteen years of pleasantness mixed with disappointment, it would already be done. That's my life. I go to school, play soccer in the rain, try to keep my parents and my best friend, Kirin, entertained—and I take a lot of bubble baths.

Yep, that's me. Birdie Sidwell: a small, brilliant person, who's no trouble at all to those around her.

Even my teachers love me. I get A's on all my stories. *Vivid*, is what they say about them. Next to my similes and metaphors they write *Original! Quirky!* Of course the stories are just practice for my book. My book will be *big*. Huge! It will have action and terror and maybe even sex! Publishers will beg me for it, movie producers will call me on their cell phones, and other bestselling authors will be my friends—

"Birdie?" Mom was tapping on the bathroom door. Her bathroom door, actually. I have my own bathroom, but hers always seems nicer. "Clean yet, honey? It's been an hour. . . . Your dad's hoping for a shower before bed."

"Clean as diamonds, Mom."

I flopped over on my stomach, sighing heavily as water lapped over the edge. "Your tub is a paradise of coconut oil."

"Yes, but you've got coconut oil in your own bathroom too."

"Yours smells better." Better than sunburned moondrops? "Mom? The floor's pretty wet in here. Dad's welcome to use my shower. . . . There might not be any more hot water, though."

"Oh, Birdie, for heaven's sake."

He won't care. He knows baths are important to me, and it's not like he has school in the morning.

"It's bedtime," Mom said. "Wipe up the floor. Put the top back on my coconut oil, if any's left."

"None is."

Mom's sigh is bigger than mine, even through a door.

Usually being my mother keeps her very content. It's being superintendent of schools, her day job, that I find a problem.

"Why not just stay home with *me*?" I've asked her a dozen times. "Make homemade angel food cake like you never do? Paint my toenails?"

She just smiles.

Fortunately Dad's home during the day, being a genius for the government. He's working on a soybean that will end world hunger. Being home gives him a chance to tend the special garden in the basement where vegetables are grown for my salads.

Along with my special baths, my special salads are my one big necessity. I used to have asthma. We were all traumatized by those times. It was actually heinous and preposterous and even gruesome, but you can't write an adventure book about asthma! My body is still behind because of it. I do a lot of things, like eating homegrown salad, so I can catch up. And I still have inhalers and meds in the medicine cabinet, just in case.

I guess it's obvious, but I've been through a lot.

○ ○ ○

One big thing I survived is when I was seven and my best friend, Kirin, was transferred out of our neighborhood school and into Nu-Way Academy, across the bridge in Washington.

Let me say first that even Mom, who thinks diversity is a good thing, says this school is radical. The "Nu" of Nu-Way comes from a guy named Nudleman who started a chain of schools.

His main idea is turning Negative Thinkers into Positive Thinkers. Which looks like it works because if kids don't instantly pretend to be thinking positively, they get *spanked*!

Hel-*lo*? How negative is that?

I've seen Nudleman in person. He walks around downtown

in his expensive regular clothes just like he was normal, except he carries a staff. He always has kids with him, who he calls his flock.

If something like a scoop of ice cream falls off a cone and splats onto one of his flock's feet, she doesn't say, "Shoot!" like a real kid. She says, "Wow! An opportunity to give my Nikes a scrub!"

Scary. And my best friend, who never did anything worse than sass her mom, was being sent there! At the time it happened, it seemed worse than a kidnapping.

Kirin came to school with me for the first week of second grade. We sat as close to each other as we could, just like in kindergarten and first grade. If she had a clue what was coming, she never said a word.

Her mother arrived early one afternoon, cracked open the classroom door as if hating to disturb. Her lipstick, as usual, was shaped into a coaxing smile.

She tiptoed in, eyes glittering with news. She handed Ms. West a yellow slip of paper, the official kind from the principal's office. Then she practically danced over to Kirin, took her small wrist inside her own plump manicured hand, and flopped her daughter's hand around at us.

"Say goodbye, Kirin."

"Mom! Let go of me right *now*—"

Kirin had always been willful. Mrs. Kimball would no doubt punish her once they were back in their car.

"Goodbye?" Ms. West was frowning at the yellow slip. "Why didn't I know anything about this?"

Mrs. Kimball's smile tightened a notch.

"Does it really mean for *good*, Mrs. Kimball?"

"It's a withdrawal slip," Mrs. Kimball said shortly. "What about that don't you understand?" Catching herself, she inflated her voice with bubbles again. "Actually, I just got the news myself! Kirin's been chosen to join her own special flock."

She beamed around at those of us not-chosen.

A flock? This was so surprising! I'd always loved animals: herds, flocks, individuals. Bugs were the only thing I didn't like to pet! But Kirin's mom never liked animals. Not even a hamster had been allowed through their polished doorway. Whenever Kirin asked for a pet, Mrs. Kimball glanced meaningfully at me.

"You have Birdie, dear. She's your pocket pal."

Hel-*lo*, Mrs. Kimball! It's not like being slightly small made me a mouse or a parakeet or something!

Way before she took Kirin away from me, I'd learned never to trust her or her carefully hidden temper. And now she was saying Kirin was leaving school to join a *flock*?

The room had gone very quiet. Kirin was everyone's princess. Each day her golden beauty radiated powerfully within the kingdom of our classroom, affecting even Ms. West.

Kirin looked made of flowers, but really she was as edgy and unpredictable as a honeybee. And we were her little bee-slaves. I knew her better than anyone: She'd been my best friend since we were old enough to play together. I was very proud of that.

Mrs. Kimball had her on her feet and was leading her away a bit too eagerly.

"*Stop* it, Mom—"

Kirin tripped at the doorway. For that moment, watching her caught inside a snowy billow of muslin, it came to me that it would be a flock of swans she would join.

I loved swans! I loved birds of all kinds! Wasn't my name Birdie? Surely that meant something!

My mouth went wide with panic. I tried to say *Take me too, I want to be in your flock! With the swans!*

But nothing came out.

The reluctant clack of Kirin's footsteps echoed down the hall. The classroom door swished closed and we were left in silence.

Ms. West did her best to make things right. "Well . . . happy trails to Kirin in her new second grade! Isn't that right, class?"

She glanced at the empty seat pushed so close to mine, and then at the inhaler that always sat on top of my desk. No doubt remembering how Kirin and I had come hand in hand the first day of school. A blond princess, and a small girl buttoned inside a sweater the exact same red as her hair.

A medical card had been pinned to me like a badge: *Asthma precipitated by excessive emotion, exercise, and certain allergens.*

But for once I didn't need my inhaler. Inside my mind, a story was forming. I too was a swan. I breathed deeply as I beat across a pink-streaked sky, keeping a close eye on the snowy, outspreading flock. I was not the leader—Kirin was the leader—but I was also not a pocket pal.

I was definitely keeping up with the others!

o o o

That was six years ago. It didn't take long for me to figure out that Kirin merely changed schools. I shouldn't say merely, I mean it was Nu-Way. But, for a while, I saw a lot less of her. Mrs. Kimball had plans for her daughter, for "straightening her out"—like bends and curves were bad things! And the plans didn't include me.

The Nu-Way across the bridge only went up to sixth grade, so starting last year, Kirin and I were back together again in seventh grade at Riverton Middle School.

She's still beautiful, but now it's like she's a flower from the florist shop instead of from a fairy woodland.

I imagined the Nu-Way teachers and Mrs. Kimball taking turns flyswatting at her honeybee spirit until it turned waspy and mean. Now her sting is hidden deep inside her smiles and faultless phrasing. Sometimes I think I'm the only one who notices. Maybe that's why I get stung the most.

On weekends her mother drives the two of them back over the bridge for tea at Nudleman's house. It's supposed to be an honor; only the most special of his flock get invited. But I know it's all about keeping Kirin *straightened out*.

I wish she could have escaped back at the very beginning. Flown off with the flock of swans that had seemed so vivid to me. But how could she? She was just a little girl, and the swans were just a story.

I still call her my best friend, but my true best friend disappeared forever down the hall that day.

I've lived in Riverton, Oregon, since I was born. Most of the houses here are old and grand, built when our town was rich from the long-ago days of trapping and timbering and salmon fishing. Now we're basically known for rain. Fall, winter, and spring are the seasons of rain. Summer is the season of not-as-much-rain.

I'm in eighth grade now. It's spring, and it's raining. I've filled out some since outgrowing asthma, and I've gotten almost average at sports. I still do my best thinking in warm water, and I've perfected the indoor cartwheel.

This morning, I was late getting downstairs for school. Mom left a warm breakfast burrito for me and went on to work. Dad was working in a nearby corner of the house, clickity-clacking away on his laptop.

I chomped at the burrito, buttoned my sweater, and peeked out the arched parlor window. When it's not storming, drizzling, misting, or fogged in, we have a view clear across the river to the mountains of Washington. Ships from all over the world enter the Columbia River here, then slide silently on to Portland. When the windows are open at night, I fall asleep to their foghorns and the bark of restless sea lions. All my life, it's been like this.

Today the view was pure April: dense, steady gray rain. Kirin came up the block looking tall, slender, and impatient. She halted briefly on the sidewalk, shook her head, and ran up the porch steps.

I opened the door and said, "Rain," as if that were another

way of saying hello, then stuffed a chunk of burrito in my mouth.

She said, "Late," and propped her dripping umbrella against the parlor wall.

She likes me to be totally ready and standing on the porch so she can get to school early, hang out with the football boys. Since she's a cheerleader, she feels a constant need to cheer them with her presence.

I rummaged inside the front closet. The high-wattage bulb did its best to cast an encouraging light over the litter of drab rain gear. I couldn't find a single pair of shoes that wouldn't feel like wearing damp baby seals.

My dad calls Oregon the Great North Wet. I used to think that was funny but now I think it sucks. Life for a thirteen-year-old girl shouldn't be all about rain.

I said exactly this to Kirin.

"Life for a thirteen-year-old girl shouldn't be all about rain." Mistake. Now she'd just say it's *not* all about rain.

"What do you call our soccer team?" she said. "Do you call it *rain*?" Her whole tawny-blond face tightens up when she tries to smile at the same time as being peeved. "Am *I* rain? Is the Cloud Dance rain? Why do you like to act like everything in Riverton is boring—"

"Actually, the Cloud Dance *is* about rain, Kirin. I'm not saying rain's a bad thing." I gestured grandly around the parlor like it was the whole world. "It's lush and green in Riverton, no one gets sunburned, we have umbrella shops up the gazoo—"

"Ga-*zoo*? Do you mean butt? Umbrellas . . . *up the butt*? That's a highly negative image, Birdie. You know I don't want negative images in my head!"

Her voice rose on the last point, making it clear I'd thrown her positive intentions to the dogs.

I swear Nu-Way permanently ruined the part of her that used to be so special. Now, it was mostly soccer and being neighbors that kept us together. And my endless fascination that someone can look like a blond diva and have the personality of an aging meter maid.

"*Gazoo*'s not a swearword," I said. "And even if it does mean butt, butts are an essential part of the human anatomy. . . ."

My voice trailed off as she reached past me for the new green rain slicker gleaming on its hanger that Mom just got me at Nordstroms. Kirin shrugged out of her own wet jacket and pulled it on, admiring herself in the long mirror inside the closet door. She flicked her gorgeous blond hair back over the hood.

I was the skinny girl who stood behind her in the mirror, admiring her in spite of myself. I was the one who tried harder than anyone to look like Nicole Kidman, my all-time most favorite Australian citizen even though I haven't been allowed to watch about half her movies. I had long red curls and pale skin, but no real hope of ever being tall or sexy.

Really, I looked more like a Raggedy Ann doll.

"Can I wear this?" Kirin's voice goes all little-girlish when she wants a favor. "My raincoat's getting crackles, and besides I love teal. My eyes are teal." She smiled at her eyes in the mirror.

They *were* teal, and large, and bright with enthusiasm for how she looked in my slicker.

She glanced at me and said, as if she were forgiving me instead of borrowing something, "Just try not to be a Negative Thinker . . . ?"

I shook my head. I heard this at least once every single morning.

I laced my feet into my driest pair of Docs, pushed the loose spirals of hair back from my face, and grabbed my old yellow rain slicker from a hook. Not that Kirin noticed, but it was stiff as well as cracked.

"You can wear my new slicker for *one day*, Kirin; then you have to give it back."

Why did I always give in to her? Or confide in her? I wish I'd never mentioned rain! For a minute I felt my chest tightening up the way it used to do. In the beginning, it was Kirin's mother who'd had that effect on me. Now it was Kirin herself.

I breathed carefully, imagined the relaxing smell of coconuts, and opened the front door.

"Bye, Dad," I called into the house.

"Be careful," he called back.

His usual goodbye.

"I will."

My usual answer, even though I never especially *was* careful, since there was nothing in Riverton to be careful of.

I swallowed the last cold (yuck) bite of burrito and pushed out the door, books slip-sliding in my arms.

Kirin stood on the porch a moment, giving the world a

chance to be dazzled. She folded her hair into the slicker's hood so it would stay glossy and straight, adjusted her silvery backpack for maximum waterproofness, then rushed into the rain as though speed would somehow get her to school less wet.

Kirin's life was also about rain, but I didn't plan to share that information with her.

o o o

A bunch of us were huddled outside the school after soccer practice. The season is over, but we practice year-round to keep our endurance up. The Ducks are famous for their endurance—go, Ducks!—in an Oregon-northern-coast sort of way.

Today was one of those days that seemed too dark for spring. Mom's Volvo, silver-blue as the rain itself, suddenly appeared through the downpour, pulled alongside the curb. Its powerful wake made kids squeal and jump back or be drenched.

Kirin gasped like Mom was a maniac driver.

"Bye, Keers. I need my raincoat back tomorrow." She gave me a blank look and I turned to call up the steps, "Bye, Coach Stinson."

The coach squinted back through the rain. "Bye-bye, Birdie."

I hated it when anyone said that, never knowing if it was innocent or if they were making the usual feeble joke about my name and the Broadway musical. I was pretty sure Coach Stinson wouldn't tease me.

She stooped for a glimpse of Mom inside the station wagon. "Put ice on that knee—and say hello to your mother."

Being Riverton's superintendent of schools gets Mom, and me, a lot of notice from the teachers.

I could feel Kirin waiting for me to offer a ride, but today I didn't feel like sharing my mom. I slipped inside the warm car, smelled the fresh, grassy scent she always wears.

"Go, Ducks!" she said.

"Go, Ducks." My response was anything but spirited. "My life's about rain, Mom."

"Yes, honey, it is."

I smiled. Leave it to her to be honest.

"This is Riverton." She drove slowly down the street. "All our lives are about rain. But! In two months, for this particular outstandingly lucky family, life will be . . . what?"

"Golden sunshine, endless adventure, and the best year of our lives!" Mom nodded. *Yes!* Only two months, and all our years of planning would come true!

I punched on the radio. I could count on Mr. Wynn for some sunny tunes. He was the school's new music teacher and afterschool disk jockey. Bob Marley was singing that song about three little birds sitting on his doorstep, telling him don't worry—

"*'Cause every little thing gonna be all right. . . .*"

Mom hummed along, unpinning her long dark hair, which had a new and interesting sheen this year: a little bit of gray creeping in. She shook it out like she was already on St. Petts and feeling the sunshine.

In my opinion my parents were way cooler people than any of my friends' thirty-something parents. Mine even went to Berkeley at the best time: the seventies. Well, Mom went. Dad taught there.

In her college pictures, Mom is shapely and beautiful, hair parted in the middle, flipped up on the ends. In my favorite snapshot she's standing in front of a Jimi Hendrix poster, posed like she's playing an invisible guitar. She's supercool in her wrinkle-free, wide-collared polyester jacket. Plaid bell-bottoms flare over chunky platform shoes. Dad was no doubt wowed by her.

I noticed lately she was looking more like those young pictures. Definitely slimmer after a winter of Weight Watchers and Nordic Track. Once she gets an idea going, that's it.

"You're getting skinny, Mom!"

"Skin and bones." She smiled, her pink cheeks going pinker. "When I dive into those warm, crystal blue seas, my bathing suit's just going to drop off me—"

"Give the sea turtles an eyeful— Hey, there's Dad!"

His umbrella bobbed along the side of the street ahead of us. I knew he was working as he walked. He spends night and day living inside rows, columns, *clouds* of numbers. I may be brilliant, but I'm not brilliant enough to know—yet—how soybeans can be turned into numbers, and then into something that will help with world hunger.

That takes a genius. Serious magazines write serious articles about Henry Sidwell (my dad) and his bean formula. Every two weeks the U.S. of A. pays him a salary for his latest calculations on engineering a soybean that's going to be so big and so strong, it will one day be grown in deserts and on mountaintops all over the world. Everyone will have something to eat.

I mean, it's not pizza, but imagine how terrible it would be if you had a little girl and there was no food in your town, and your yard was so hard and dusty that there was no chance of growing anything to feed her. Then one day you got special seeds that would grow soybean plants with just a tiny bit of water. All kinds of food can be made from soybeans. You'd be able to feed your little girl, and she'd have a chance to grow up like the rest of us do.

That's how Mom explains Dad's work to me.

Several afternoons a week he has conference calls with the guys at the Department of Agriculture. They grow the beans he's engineered, report the results of each crop. Every once in a while, Dad flies to Washington, D.C., and once, when he was on TV, he sat in the same room as the president!

Somehow everyone in Riverton missed that program. Here he's just the guy who stays home and takes care of his daughter while his wife runs the school system.

"Dad!" I yelled out the window.

"Hey! Darned if it's not my family!"

He hopped into the backseat, giving the impression he was spry at an advanced age, only his age isn't advanced at all. He's just one of those small slender people who never looks either young or old, but is somehow always in pretty good shape. Because of his nose, he's not 100% handsome. It was a large feature even when he used to have hair on his head. Mom kisses him on the nose a lot. I used to think this was to make it better, but now

I suspect it's because she thinks it's cute. Which it is, really. If you're a dad.

But not if you're a female kid. I touched my own nose. So far it resembled Mom's: small and manageable. But like the rest of me, it could still transform. When I was little, my hair was silky-straight just like hers. Then at ten, here came the curls. Dad used to have curly red hair, so I'm living with a lot of unknowns here.

Having a large nose is near the top of my list of the worst things that could possibly happen.

Suddenly I felt cartwheels building up inside me. The living room was specially arranged so I could do three in a row. When we got home, I'd ask Mom and Dad if they could sit on the couch and watch me for a while.

chapter

2

morgan

I am not like others. My habits are carved from the rituals of living at sea. My speech is marked from being a reader more than a speaker, and from never having lived in any of the countries whose languages I understand.

When I was eleven, I went to an American disco on the island of Martinique. The way I dance takes up a lot of room. It was as if I were the wheel and the boy I danced with the hub. He chopped his legs in place, his eyes never leaving my abdomen.

"Yeah, baby, oh, baby—" he shouted redundantly. "Oh, baby, you *go!*"

The music was very loud, its deep notes intensifying the beat of my heart.

I spun close and spoke into his ear: "I prefer you not to address me as 'baby.' We had a baby in our family and it was born lifeless. I prefer you to refer to me as preadolescent."

He frowned and shouted back through the music, "Where are you from, Mars?"

"No." I frowned back, then caromed against his shoulder. "The climate of Mars is inhospitable."

He ducked under my spiraling arms and left me to dance on my own.

I know now that the climate of discos, and many other places, is inhospitable as well.

o o o

I was nine when my sister fell from the mainsail mast, tumbled slower than time through the salty air. Her eyes, *knowing*, found me on the bowsprit and told me what she was thinking: *Wasn't this bound to happen?*

The sea leaped, opened its mouth, and ate her.

Our mother's face was wide with horror but I was the one who screamed *Oona!*

The deck lurched as the wave took her inside and swallowed her, digesting the immeasurable future of a twelve-year-old life.

Our father bounded up from the companionway, *knowing*, and stared as the wave moved in front of us, rearing with the dignity of a breaching whale.

He had been working below at the electronic weather station. Headphones dangled from his neck and broken loops of cord dragged behind him.

He tore at them, hoarse sounds coming from his throat as the wave sped off with his daughter.

"Follow it!" Father bellowed to Mother. "Turn us about!"

His leap from the side was so powerful, it rocked the boat like a second, smaller rogue force.

"Oona is gone," Mother said, her voice tormented yet final. She straightened on the swaying deck, readying herself for whatever next would come.

"Gone from the boat is gone." Her words were always instructive. "Your father is not thinking. Shall I now jump to save him? And then you to save me? And we will all be gone?"

She shook her head.

I was unable to think. Should I turn the boat about? Should I stay by Mother's side? I stared overboard and it was decided for me.

Father, already too far from the boat, thrashed in a mess of hampering electrical cord.

Would we lose him as well?

I jumped to the sails. Line ripped through my hands as I reeled them tight, headed the boat toward Father, then let the sails drop into sagging bundles of cloth. We instantly slowed, floundered in place.

Mother was already over the boat's side, hanging one-armed from the rope ladder. I heard her sharply command Father to become still, to let her bring him in. She expertly extended the grappling hook with her free arm and dragged him back. He had, as she commanded, gone still as death. The sun came out and shone horribly on his face.

Holding them both to the ladder, Mother unholstered her knife and freed Father's body from the cord. He jerked himself away from her, his huge body bursting up onto the boat like Neptune from the sea.

He raced up and down the deck, but swift as our beating hearts, the wave had vanished, carrying Oona forever beyond the horizon.

The sea flattened. Father threw his head back and roared.

"You *see?*" he cried to my mother. "That this was bound to happen?"

He went below again, leaving me behind as though I were neither precious nor all that remained of his children.

He cried for days and nights.

"You *see?*" he shouted up whenever he thought to.

My mother didn't know how to cry, so she opened the medicinal rum kept for emergencies, and became drunken.

Was this also *bound to happen?*

O O O

My sister was two when our parents took to the sea. I wasn't to be born for another year, but I've heard the stories.

They were Norwegian, my parents, which doesn't explain so much. Most Norwegians live regular lives in regular houses. I've looked it up in the encyclopedias we have aboard, and I've visited www.Norway.com. I've seen for myself the images of cozy homes and snow-laden fields.

But life there did not suit my mother. She said she felt the ancestral tug of Viking blood, calling her to sea.

Maybe she did, the way she looked, tall and straight and fierce. Her lion-red hair, dull and magnificent, so unlike Father's shining fine blondness.

"I must live a free life," she said.

"A decent life," Father said. No way to know if he was disagreeing.

I could imagine him as a clean-shaven young man: a powerful, deep-voiced giant. My mother's strong features and broad shoulders, suddenly womanly in his presence. Was that why she chose him? Or was it because he had a fine business and wore a fine suit? I've seen the mildewed photographs. The two of them like stars of the Olympic Games. Unless all people are like that, in Norway.

"A free life for our children," Mother said, ". . . if we're to have them."

Having said that, did she close herself to him? The way she did to Oona and me if we hurt ourselves and cried?

Many times over, she repeated her ideas. "We must do as our ancestors did: voyage into the world, ride the warm Caribbean seas."

"Conquer and pillage?" Father asked her.

She lifted her chin and for a while was silent.

After she bore Oona she began again, only louder.

"All right then," my father said.

He sold his profitable business. Insurance, is what it was.

They were already fine sailors. They purchased a new wooden boat. It was made in an old Nordic style but outfitted with modern electronic necessities: radar, computerized weather tracking and navigation, depth sounders.

Their plan was to monitor the airways, find wealthy, hurricane-ravaged islands. They would go from island to island, and

Father would help the residents collect their insurance money, for a fee.

The family of three sailed forth and began their new life.

But the new work, the ruin and sadness, were hard on Father.

"We feed our family from the misfortune of others," he complained.

The strong bones of Mother's face showed themselves. "It is the way of people everywhere. At least our children will live knowing what is real. Nothing for them but water and sky and truth."

O O O

I was born at sea, delivered by my mother herself.

That this worked made my father happy. He began to see that a good life was possible after all.

I know these things because parents have the same conversations over and over, reviewing their pasts, dreaming their futures. On a boat, such talk cannot be kept secret from children. It's as though we're not even there.

That's how it was for us, two sets of people, the parents and the children.

Oona and I possessed the agility that comes with a life of unpredictable footing. We looked like Mother: knuckly bones, good teeth, rough hair the color of dried blood. Oona kept our hair chopped. We were ragged and tough-looking, the way Mother wanted.

Five years after me came another baby. Our mother tried to keep her cries inside. Oona and I stayed on the bowsprit all day, hoping for dolphins. Nothing passed by except stinging clouds of jellyfish.

The baby was a boy, silky-headed and beautiful, but too large. He did not make a single sound because he was not born alive. Father wrapped him up in our best Polartec blanket, as though being dead were the same as being cold, and then tenderly fed him to the sea.

My sister and I wanted to be sad, but the baby hadn't had time to be our brother.

"He looked like me!" Father cried out to no one, because Mother was down in her berth and nearly dead herself.

"He *blames* her," Oona whispered to me that night. "She didn't do it right."

Her voice was clamped and sure, as if she'd known all along such a thing was bound to happen.

I didn't know. I didn't know anything!

I nodded in the dark, believing everything she said. Only she could translate the subtle, isolated world into which I'd been born.

After the wrapped baby, Father steered a trafficked course, joining many craft headed for the commercial harbors of Venezuela. He swore as he dodged barges and cruise ships. Mother was silent as he navigated our boat alongside a crowded fueling dock. Harbor officials greeted us and helped us tie in to a slip. On either side, boats were close enough to step on to.

Father was punishing Mother.

The dock was loud and stinking. At night, steel music rose from the café, drumming sea-dreams from our heads. Dancers waved their arms and hopped in place.

Mornings, Oona and I climbed off the boat. Tabby cats and shy brown boys followed us around.

After dark, Mother and Father never allowed us to leave the boat, though they began to do so themselves.

A month passed and something happened. They started to like each other again. We heard them laughing when they came home from the café, heard them acting playful in their berth. They were more like children than we had ever been.

"It's the drums," Oona explained.

I nodded. I wouldn't have guessed such a thing.

Mother smiled freely at Father, her teeth shiny and hard as a horse's. Father rubbed her hindquarters and made the low noise of a whale.

He cut back his formidable beard and we observed that his jaw was relaxing. He monitored the storms again. One morning he unrolled the charts and a rumble softened his throat. I drew close. He looked up at me, and his eyes crinkled. This was his way of smiling. In that moment, understanding passed between us. I have no words to explain it, but it was a family-victory feeling. It had to do with Mother, and her specialness, and how the rest of us must hold together during the times when she was difficult.

He abruptly pointed here, there, with his great chin, meaning I should secure all loose possessions below.

We gathered on deck. Mother stepped from the boat, unwound dock lines, leaped back aboard as we moved off. Father motored free of the harbor. A jerk of his arm meant Oona was to raise the sails. Our boat caught the wind with a jolt and obediently heeled northwest. Father held us at 307 degrees. Off to storm-torn Jamaica!

Mother sang Viking songs in a loud voice and the wind tangled her hair into a long unfixable rope.

O O O

Nights were for learning the stars and studying our books. Once again, we slept to the strange and beautiful opera heard only when you're deep at sea. The ghosts of perished sailors, if you are to believe such things.

Days were again for play. My sister and I climbed the mainsail mast like monkeys and never, ever lost our balance.

Our parents let us be. We knew to come down if the weather turned heavy. Life returned to nonrules.

Except sometimes when our father imagined the approach of a waterspout or a rogue wave and could not restrain himself.

"Come *down!*" he would shout. "*Quickly!*"

Our mother instantly appearing at his side, a Viking goddess, her voice equal in strength to his.

"Children! No! Listen only to yourselves!"

Forced to choose whom to obey, her or our father, Oona chose Father. I chose what Oona chose.

She scrambled down the mast before me, hit the deck with ready excuses. "We came down because we wanted to come down, Mother. We were ready."

"And you?" She tilted my face up with her hand, my heart swelling to her rough affection. "Did you come because Oona did? Or because you read the skies?"

I nodded yes to both.

Father cast his eyes at the line of darkness fermenting on the horizon. A squall, coming so fast the sky blackened as we watched.

We harnessed ourselves, snapped our lines to the boat, eased the sails.

Mother strode to the helm, braced herself, kept us headed to 307 degrees. Our boat went rail down. The drag of the sea on the wheel was too much even for her muscled shoulders. Father took over and stood double watch.

The companionway door was shut against a broaching sea. Below, in the dark, Mother and Oona and I breathed the smothering air and were fitful. Mother read by flashlight, eyes jacking side to side like caged mongooses. Oona and I braced against the lee wall of our berth, the sea pounding in our ears, pounding to be let in.

Then it was gentle morning, the night just one of thousands we'd survived. Our boat had done what it did best: stayed unbroken in a world of punishment.

Three hundred seven degrees, corrected five degrees this way, three back again. Oona read the stars and whispered to me: "We're nearly to Jamaica!"

She stayed up the mast all day, waiting. Her patience was a trial for me. I descended and made my way to the fore of the boat, to the very tip of the bowsprit. Sitting sideways, the rail formed a guard around me. My legs dangled free between stanchions. I called out for dolphins and they came like jets. Inside our bow wave, their faces were stiff with laughter.

Suddenly a cloud passed beneath the sun. The dolphins, *knowing*, fled with the light.

"No!" I cried. Not so soon!

But dolphins know things even Vikings can't know. Oona told me that.

Rogue energy left over from the previous day's storm burst fantastically from the sea.

O O O

The wave came at us from behind. Father was below, Mother at the helm, Oona's gaze fixed on the forward horizon: all of them unaware. It loomed over the boat, broke against us with such violence that Mother was thrown against the bulkhead, her teeth and cheekbone shattering.

I wrapped myself around the rail, riding the boat as it rose into the air. When it crashed back to sea, the mast bowed like a catapult and flung my sister free. As she tumbled, what seemed strangest was that her dull, dried-blood hair shone bright as a halo. She turned her head, looking at me as the sea caught her in its mouth and took her forever from sight.

Oona!

For a while, the ship wallowed stupidly as it tried to pilot itself. We drifted away from Jamaica, circling, circling the empty plains of the sea.

My father's beard grew down to his waist, and he became permanently silent. My mother, her wounded face yet fiercer and more wondrous, became drunken and stayed so.

But the boat was too small for solitary drunkenness, and soon my father joined in. The rum-laden air cloaked the boat and turned it sluggish. I climbed the mast where the breeze was fresh and normal. There I looked for land, and for Oona.

In this manner my parents grew old, and I grew older. More and more they docked, seeking out taverns and the presence of others like them.

When they went ashore in Panama, beckoned by rum and rusting steel drums, I sailed away without them.

Now I circle the ocean alone, the child of a Viking mother. I listen only to myself, but the voice I hear is Oona's.

Another of the things I've survived also has to do with Kirin.

Have I mentioned that last year my breasts started up? Not in a big way, but a little something was happening. I was sensitive about it, partly because anything at all was there, and partly because it was hardly anything. It's complicated. But then I got to thinking about Mom's full-blown bosoms and what a part of the family they'd always been—I don't mean like *pocket pals*—but they were one of her nice, comforting features, and attractive in a motherly way. Dad keeps a picture out that shows her when she was young and wearing a bathing suit. I wouldn't mind looking like that! Anyway, she didn't always have them and then she did, and I saw that it worked out fine.

But once you're in middle school, you don't want to have anything noticeable or new that isn't already 100% fabulous.

I was only a seventh grader then. There are probably a lot of ways of managing new breasts, but I went for invisibility.

And I was getting away with it, until the day my T-shirt got wet on the way to school and my new bra showed through in living detail. That was not fun, especially after Kirin got involved.

I was running late for school. Kirin had gotten a ride with her mom. Mrs. Kimball parked in front of my house for about one minute, honking on and on while I frantically motioned just-a-minute-just-a-minute! through the window.

By the time I ran out, they were gone.

It was warm and hazy so I didn't bother with a rain jacket. In Riverton, rain can come from nowhere, and that's of course what happened. The bra showing through wouldn't have been so bad, I mean Madonna lightened everyone up about bras a long time ago. But I wasn't Madonna, and I didn't need a bra, not at all, and thanks to the rain, that showed too.

It was Kirin who got the world to notice.

"Hey, Birdie!" She stood dry and perfect under the school's sheltered entryway. Most of the football team stood around her. Before-school practice had been washed out once again. Max, star of the team and Kirin's potential new love-slave, hovered next to her.

As soon as she spied me, she yelled, "Birdie!" and started an urgent little dance in place, like she had to go to the bathroom. "Since you're already wet, would you go get my makeup bag? In Mom's car? Pretty please?"

Max was grinning down at her as if looking like you have to pee is adorable. I guess it is, if you're Kirin.

Apparently my soggy biology notebook was doing a good job of hiding my chest.

I saw Kirin's mother's black BMW way down the block, crouching like a waterproof panther inside its swirl of exhaust. The car was a present from her father, who I'd seen about six times since I was born. He was *always* on a business trip somewhere, or at home "recovering" from his last trip.

Behind the swipe of windshield wipers, Mrs. Kimball waggled a little pink bag at me. An expensive Le Cosmétique makeup kit, the kind you can only get at city stores.

I sighed and trudged toward the car.

"Nice bra, Birdie," Kirin called. "Didn't know you had one."

Max said, "Didn't know you *needed* one!"

I heard him, and so did the whole football team. It was apparently the funniest thing imaginable.

Mrs. Kimball's dark window rolled silently down. She gazed at my dripping, pouting face and pooched her lips in mock sympathy.

"Positive thoughts, Birdie!"

"I'm not a Nu-Wayian, Mrs.—"

My words ricocheted off the closing window.

I trotted the bag back to Kirin, who had her lips pooched exactly like her mother.

Boys I'd known since kindergarten smiled down on me.

"Just kidding, Birdie. We like you how you are—"

"Yeah—you'll be Queen of the Cloud Dance when you grow up—"

"Grow up you-know-where!" The quarterback held cupped hands up to his chest, hooted like an ape.

"Birdie?" Kirin said in that coaxing-mother voice of hers. "Little pocket pal? Do I see a smile?"

Little pocket pal? We were in middle school now!

I tried to tug her away to a quiet corner, but she wasn't about to give up her queen-bee position. "Hel-*lo,* Kirin Kimball!" I whispered. "Why are you calling me *pocket pal* in front of the guys? Did I not just bring your makeup bag as a big favor?"

She answered in her cheerleading voice, "Not a favor, Birdie! An opportunity! To help another person!"

"Kirin, you are exactly like your mother."

Her face twisted up the way it does when she forces it to smile. I knew what I'd said was cruel, but she didn't disagree. She just laughed it off.

"Why, thank you! I'm sure that's the best you can do for a positive thought."

I pushed inside the building, my T-shirt wet, revealing, and smudged with ink from my notebook. But without Kirin to point it out, no one else even noticed.

I survived being embarrassed and being angry. But I was left permanently sad at what had happened between us. After all, Kirin was the girl I called my best friend.

Did I pretend we were as close as we had been in second grade because everyone thought she was so special? Because others thought I must be special if we were best friends?

All I knew was that she was beautiful but she wasn't a nice person.

All I knew was it had been over a long time and neither of us could admit it.

o o o

I was three when I had my first asthma attack. Either I remember how I was before then, or I've put it together with the pictures I've seen so many times.

I was a plump little thing. In one photo, I'm running along a rocky beach, a tiny vacation house right on the Pacific Ocean. It's like I'm throwing myself through space. I'm laughing and I'm happy and I look like I'm made of peaches. My hair's still glossy smooth and bobbed short. I can tell that I have my parents' entire attention, something I still like to have whenever possible.

After that, after my asthma started, the pictures begin to feature a quiet life. I am the thin redhead sitting next to a girl whose hair looks like combed sunshine (guess who?), as we cut out paper dolls in my room. Another shows me watering the basement garden inside the shelter of my daddy's arms. One is of Dr. Bennett, making one of his famous house calls. All of us are smiling like he's there for a tea party instead of with one of the shots that let me breathe again.

In fifth grade, I decorated a frame with seashells for my favorite photo: me and Mom and Fat Silly, our tabby cat who made me wheeze but who we kept until he died of old age. The three of us are curled up reading a book together on the upstairs window seat. The light's perfect. Mom's and my skin creamy as pearls, the shadows around my eyes somehow old-fashioned and pretty. If you look close, Dad's there too, his face and the camera reflected on the windowpane.

It's just the way I like things, all of us together.

○ ○ ○

Mom was thirty-seven when I was born, and my dad was I don't know how old. He looks the same in all the pictures, like he was never a boy or any special age. It's weird I don't know and don't ask him. Like not wanting to know Santa Claus's age or something.

My parents being older, and me being the only child, set our family apart.

It's never been clear to me if I was all the children my parents wanted or all they could handle. Not that I'm any trouble! I'm not! I'm a little picky about food is all. I know it's hard to find ginger ice cream. Except for that, I just need the regular new clothes everyone does and piano and dance and diving lessons and getting to soccer games and sleepovers and being driven to the pool or the movies and sometimes having appointments with the doctor. That's it.

I'm easy, just like I always tell Mom when she's fixing my special salad.

"Birdie, you want your baby carrots sliced diagonally or lengthwise tonight?"

"Either way. I'm easy."

Just as long as she doesn't slice them straight across! Something about straight across just ruins a salad for me!

The only other thing is that I like to get picked up exactly on time after school, which Mom totally doesn't mind.

Any more than Dad minds growing lettuce and tomatoes for my salads, down in the little greenhouse he set up in the basement.

He's always saying, "This is the last season, Birdie—you're well now. We can get all this stuff at the farmers' market!"

We *can't,* though; who has white-striped radishes in January? Besides, it's good for Dad to take time out from thinking about soybeans and energy and work, even Mom says that.

Of course I also like for my parents to listen carefully to what happens to me every day—they want to know!—and to look at anything I might have written or drawn. I like that to happen at dinnertime. Sometimes I give a quiz if I think Dad isn't paying attention or if Mom starts sighing.

After homework, if Mom's not doing her own work on the computer, it's video time! Sometimes I can get Dad to sit with us, but he still brings his laptop.

Before bed, there's my cup of ginger ice cream, and then my bubble bath. I have a collection of fragrances: rose, lavender, peppermint, coconut. Mom has an even bigger collection, although her bottles run empty fast since I mostly use her tub.

My bedtime is late for my age, eleven o'clock, because after the bath of course I need to write stories using all the fresh ideas that came from the bubbly water. We all think eleven's too late, but that's just part of the price of being Birdie Sidwell.

To sum it up, I suspect if my parents thought they could have had several children that were just as easy as me, they naturally would have had them. Maybe it's that they got too old for more. It's another of the things I don't ask about.

No doubt the loneliness of not having sisters and brothers has helped make me the interesting person I am.

○ ○ ○

Mom is a natural-born teacher and a natural-born boss. She went to school to do exactly what she does, which is run a small city school system. When she gets dressed in her trim gabardines, her glimmery silks and glossy leather shoes, you'd never know that inside she's dancing to a reggae beat.

She's devoted to her job and to Riverton but both things cause her to sigh in the winter, when days are shortest and wettest.

Many times over, she's repeated her ideas at the dinner table.

"Someday we'll leave this all behind and go for a long vacation. A warm dry Caribbean place where they've never heard of soybeans or asthma or school bonds."

I'm thinking, *Yes!*

"Hey—I for one don't mind it here," Dad would say, suddenly alerted by no-soybeans talk. He'd wink at me and add, "Here in the Great North Wet."

"I know, Henry. But you wouldn't mind it *there,* either. For a while?"

He'd glance at his laptop for reassurance. "Oh, sure, for a while, no, that's fine, Clara. For a while . . ."

Then finally they'd be ready to hear what I'd learned in English.

They know how to be laid-back; they're just out of practice, working so long to make a difference.

Just after Mom graduated from college and Dad quit his teaching job, they were farmers of some sort in Hawaii. Or maybe that was their version of a honeymoon.

Then Mom spent years working with the schools on a dusty reservation in New Mexico. I don't know much about that except something big happened there, between Dad and an ancient Anasazi bean. Mom said he'd sit between the rows of spotted beans and just *think*.

All those thoughts led him to some unique conclusions, and before long the government hooked up with him. Then my parents looked around for the perfect place to raise a perfect child, and it's been me and Riverton ever since.

The plan has always been for Mom to reach her fifteen-year mark as superintendent so she could take a year off and still have her job waiting for her when she got back.

Dad's job will always be there. As long as he has his laptop and perfects his soybean, he gets paid.

My job is to be ahead of my level so it will be easy for Mom to homeschool me for our year away.

In a lot of ways, even though Mom started the dream, I'm the one who wants it most. From the beginning, Dr. Bennett said the dampness of Riverton, the famous "Riverton mold," did nothing to help my asthma. Maybe a year of sunshine would make me grow like one of Dad's bean plants. I still have that daydream where I'm one of the swans and I've caught up with everyone.

○ ○ ○

The asthma started with a full-on attack. Everyone remembers the day, but Kirin and I were the only ones who saw what happened. And I guess I'm the only one who remembers. We've never talked about it.

It was summer. Mom walked me down the street to Kirin's and left me there to play in her backyard. Our cat, Fat Silly, had followed behind us. Mrs. Kimball worked under a shady tree, fussing over pots of flowers. She was fully outfitted with garden gloves, a hat, and a shiny trowel.

Kirin and I were playing in the very clean sandbox when Fat Silly jumped in with us. He dug around with unmistakable purpose, even to three-year-olds. Mrs. Kimball glanced up from her potted begonias and actually *screamed* when she saw a cat scooping away in her sandbox.

We screamed back, delighted at the sandstorm, the air above us violently festooned with sprays of sand.

Mrs. Kimball's face clamped with rage. I'd never seen rage before, and never wanted to again.

It was like she had been a marine, is how ready she was for such an outrage. She lifted an entire pot of begonias and hurled them at the cat. Fat Silly just squatted there not believing his eyes as the enormous pot came sailing—not at him, but at us! Directly at our heads!

"*Duck,* Kirin!" Mrs. Kimball shrieked. Her face bulged with horror, knowing the pot could split open the head of her own three-year-old child.

Neither Kirin nor I moved. We were as frozen in that sandbox as if it were concrete.

It landed *whunk!* directly between us, broken stems splayed out from the half-buried pot. Scarlet petals spattered our chubby shoulders like blood and fell across our chubby legs.

Fat Silly, having no taste for violence, excused himself and disappeared into the hedge.

The missile attack turned our screams from gleeful to hysterical. Mrs. Kimball scurried to undo what she had done, pluck-pluck-plucking the petals off us, tossing the pot into a wheelbarrow, smoothing the sand crater into unblemished perfection.

In a low, rushed voice she said, "Nothing happened, what's all this fuss, nothing *hap*pened."

She wiped her hands, stood, and was suddenly calm. "No cats in our yard, Birdie, you know that. A rule is a rule."

She strode to the kitchen and brought back Popsicles, which did the trick for quieting Kirin. I also went silent, but not from sucking on a cherry Popsicle. I was breathless, head tipped back, gasping for air. And then I was blue, eyes popping, and Mrs. Kimball was pressing her fat lips over my mouth, blowing in bologna-scented air, dragging me inside to dial 911.

Mom met us at the hospital.

Mrs. Kimball told her she'd tossed her straw hat at Fat Silly, filthy thing, doing his business right there in Kirin's sandbox!

43

And poor little Birdie with her fragile nervous system had simply *freaked out*! I remember her holding Kirin on her hip as she spoke. Kirin was too old for a pacifier but she chomped on one as if she could suck her way out of shock. We stared at each other. I think that's the moment we bonded, too young for words, for explaining what had happened.

Our hearts, right then, set to the exact same rhythm.

That's the day the asthma started, and that's the day when Kirin and I became best friends. Closer than friends, whatever the word for that is. I was never lonely after that. At least not until Nu-Way.

Except for the first attack, my asthma's always been controlled. It's gone now but I've still got an inhaler, pills to back it up, and the close watch of my parents and teachers.

It's supposed to be why I'm on the small side, although that could come naturally from my dad.

My name came from him as well, not, as everyone assumes, because I look like a little birdie. I'd just as soon they *did* assume that, since my real name is *Birdwinkle*. After Bivens Birdwinkle, an obscure horticulturist from some other era. Just try looking him up: Unless you're in a science library or a bean museum you won't find a thing about him.

Still, he's Dad's hero and I've got his name, so that's that.

In the beginning before Dad insisted on doing his research at home, he had to fly back and forth to Washington, D.C., every week. He was supposed to set up programs to feed other countries. He said this was an impossible task, that we needed to set up countries to feed themselves. Doing this depended on solutions he was still working on. It was hard on him. I've heard the quiet talk.

"We're feeding our family from the misfortune of others," he complained to Mom. "All this money being paid to us when there are so many out there starving, waiting for me to find a way to fix things."

Mom would say, "Mmm. It is sad, Henry. But you *are* fixing things, and at least our own child will be raised knowing how it really is, the hunger and poverty."

"How can she know? She thinks hunger is when there's no ginger ice cream in the freezer. It's only stories."

"No, Henry." I imagined her shaking her head. "I've explained it to her, she understands more than you think. Anyway, we can't deprive her to make a point. *We* weren't deprived, Henry, and we care." She sighed. "Sometimes I'd like to forget about the real world for a while, sail away, be who we are outside of working and teaching. . . ."

"But, Clara, that's who we are, aren't we? Workers and teachers?"

"I mean just for a while, Henry."

"Oh."

Sometimes I wish I *did* know about hunger and poverty. Don't forget, I'm always on the search for things heinous, preposterous, or even gruesome. I'm not just a girl who can do a perfect cartwheel. I'm an authoress of the future.

chapter

4

It had come to pass: I was leaving my parents behind. I stood ready at the helm, my tethered sailboat quivering in a warm breeze, poised for freedom. Behind me the twilight had turned the sea a pink-tipped black. Before me the harbor lights twinkled on a few at a time. I watched my parents cross the dock, making their way from the boat to the marina bar. A shanty, really, palm trees drooping at the doorway as though incurably drunken.

The wooden walkways of our boat slip rested just above the water and came close along either side of our sailboat. When I slackened the last line to the dock, we bumped softly to the left. Mother, at the same moment, swayed against Father, then away again.

This strong-willed woman, perhaps the strongest who ever lived, had never needed the safety of land or of another person, or of intoxicating drink. Things had changed for her after the death of her baby and her eldest daughter. Things had changed for all of us. Her storms were within her now, and never slackened in their rage. This freest of people was now forever anchored to places and others, by the habit of rum.

Her only rule had been "Listen to yourself."

I learned to do so.

Last month Father fell asleep on his midnight watch, unmindful of the silent cargo ship that crossed our path until its wake nearly toppled him—all of us!—overboard.

And a year and half ago, Mother, barely knowing what she did, attacked the boarding coast guard like a banshee, turning a routine inspection into a grave predicament. Only our money saved Mother from jail and the sure death of her spirit.

Had the officials known I was only sixteen, I would have been removed from my parents' custody. Luckily the coast guard assumed I was older, a hired crew member, and never asked for a birth certificate or passport; documents I am not even sure exist.

I watched my parents make these mistakes, and many others. I had listened to myself, and now I was leaving them in safer quarters.

Steel drums suddenly clattered to life inside the bar. I lifted my head.

"Good night, child."

My father's goodbye call was heavy as the tropical dusk. He cocked his head briefly my way, a small familiar gesture. In that second, and even from that distance, I believe he noticed: the corner of a sail, one small scarf, had been raised on a rigging as well known to him as his hand.

If he saw I was preparing to leave, he accepted it.

I felt the breeze shift. I was not like the others, the learned sailors, who needed engines in tight places. I lifted a bit more cloth to the wind, tossed the last line onto the dock, and silent as a foot slipped from a shoe, we backed away from the dock.

If my mother had felt the sudden distance, I believe her craggy face would have twisted into a smile, the broken teeth sharp as a cannibal's. She'd raised me to do exactly what I was doing. Pain and happiness were all the same to her: It was making your own choices that mattered.

I nodded to their familiar backs, to the harbor lights, the sound of steel music and land's slovenly ways. With a single spin of the wheel we were pointed away from the slip, the hated stall, and toward the infinite black horizon.

Hand over hand, lively as an octopus, I raised the staysail.

"Holy smokes!" a learned sailor cried from the deck of his anchored boat. "Look at that, Charlie!" His crewmate stopped to stare. "Ever see a sail go up like that? . . . Whoa, is that a *girl*?"

The boat caught the wind and I was off.

In the morning, I would crop my hair close to my head so it would be unaffected by salt and wind. What had I been thinking to let it grow below my jaw, to comb it every day as though it were a pet? Land-living does that, even to me.

Before my sister, Oona, went inside the sea, our family worked ashore for many days at a time. During hurricane season, we would sail to islands damaged by winds or floods. The wealthy islands were of course best for Father's business. He would trim his beard, put on a fresh shirt and one of his elegant tropical suit jackets. We were dazzled by his tall blond solemn-faced handsomeness. There was a black leather satchel he always took with him, and a clipboard held in the official way he had. Then he'd pick his way through the debris, working outward from the smashed, tree-strewn villages. Patiently, he would document the ruins with photographs, write each detail on his clipboard.

Nights on board would be spent arranging fair settlements for residents from their insurance companies. Batteries and computers kept us hooked into that world and made us the money we needed.

It was of course only the lucky ones, those with wealth, who had insurance. The others became Oona's and my "clients."

We'd invented our own job, packing powdered milk and beans and rice and first aid supplies from the boat into a worn green canvas sack. We would lug it to the unlucky noninsured, their shanties often in the jungly inlands or dotted along rocky, undesirable beaches. We could not offer money or housing, but we had the small necessities.

We wore our own business coats, rumpled plaid or seersucker Sunday school jackets dragged from the clothes bins of island stores with names like Mr. Boy-Clothings or Mr. Fine-n-Dandee.

That we insisted on buying and wearing these jackets, copying Father, always brought one of Mother's rare smiles: the sun breaking through her storm-cloud face.

Presented properly, we usually got our way.

"We require paint and brushes and paper, Mother, for developing our abilities." Oona would speak formally and look straight into Mother's auburn eyes.

"Oh? And who decided you need such things?"

"We decided ourselves."

"And who decided for you, Morgan? Was it Oona?" tilting my head up to read my face. I was awestruck by my mother. Awestruck, too often, by everyday life.

"No, Mother. My own self. Decided."

"Hmm. Then I expect to see you using these expensive supplies."

I watched Oona, nodded vigorously along with her.

By the same method, we were allowed to store additional supplies on board and then distribute them. The provisions were handed directly to other children, who didn't question the oddness of our mission. We also knew how to bandage cuts and how to use our sailboat's single sideband radio to call for outside help or to pass messages to the distant relatives of our clients.

Our job, the earnestness with which we carried it out, was accomplished without help or suggestion from either Mother or Father. As long as we had decided it for ourselves, Mother was content.

Mother herself often refused to go ashore at all. She hated the brokenness and the chaos left by the winds. She hated that there were so many *things* on land, and that they were so breakable. Nature itself was divided for her: There were the nature of sea and the nature of land. Her nature was the nature of the sea.

She would instead furiously read the computer's instruction manuals or scrub and polish the teakwood deck or change the engine's oil: tasks that subdued her terrible restlessness.

During the stormiest year of my childhood, the hurricane

names went all the way from Arnie to Zelda. Hurricane Hannah, the worst of them, stripped a small French island of its fabulous vacation homes. We were required to stay there long enough to grow our hair to unfamiliar lengths. Oona loved to tinker with our shaggy burnt-colored manes. She made tight little braids all over her head and then did the same to me.

She spoke in French as she wrenched my hair around. *"Reste tranquille!" Be still.* She was already as rough as Mother. "I'm making you nice."

I wanted to be nice. By looking at her I saw what I would look like: grubby sun-browned face with auburn eyes, heavy straight-across brows, and dull sprouts of red-brown hair tied up with string. Very nice. I clenched my eyes and let her finish.

Beyond our stylish new hair, we weren't distinguishable as either girls or boys. Other children were clearly a certain sex, you could see that at first glance. We understood this was important and even charming, on land. To show right away that you were girl or boy, and to keep showing it in every action. The black or brown or tan-skinned girls wore colorful ribbons and looked at us with flirting sideways glances. The boys approached with rough menace, even to say hello, and kept stocking caps tight over their hair no matter the heat.

Oona and I noticed these things, but we knew not to copy them. Mother wouldn't have allowed it. We did know we were girls, but that meant to us only that we would eventually be equipped for the burden of reproduction. Mother had explained that.

"The privilege," Father said to Mother. "Surely you must

mean the *privilege* of reproducing, when you speak to your daughters of such things."

Mother stared thoughtfully at us. "I suppose it is neither thing, my children." She shrugged her broad shoulders. "Neither burden nor privilege. You will simply choose to reproduce or not."

"Babies, she means," Oona said to me under her breath. *"Do we want having babies."*

I thought we had to choose right then. I glued my eyes to Oona's face: *Would we be having babies or not?*

But then Mother picked up her wrench and returned to repairing the engine. Father went back to his papers, and Oona carelessly kicked at a passing cockroach. I drew a great breath at having the dilemma pass.

Dilemmas came frequently to me, and I supposed that would continue. At least this last one, the decision to leave my parents on land, had been resolved. They would be with their own kind, and I with mine.

But who were my kind and where might I find them? Were there any others? Or was it just me?

I didn't even know where I was headed.

Oona?

Go where you know, do what you know.

I nodded and set my course. For now, it was enough plan: tonight the sea, tomorrow morning the cutting of my hair.

The Ducks were like a way of life. We even had a motto, "You Can't Drown a Duck!" We came up with that when we played against the Bigfoots, huge girls who were total butt-kickers.

Ten minutes into our game against them, it started storming. The rain was so fierce, we were actually breathing water as we ran. No one could even see where the ball was going!

The two coaches went into a huddle, and Coach Stinson trotted back to us.

"It's up to you girls if you want to call the game," she shouted over the crash of rain. "But if we're the ones to quit, we take the loss."

We were even more stubborn than miserable. We shook our heads no.

Coach Stinson nodded.

"No way!" she hollered to the Bigfoot coach.

Rain sheeted down his cheeks and into his open mouth. "You're kidding me!" He kicked at a mud puddle for a minute and then shrugged. "Okay! Guess you can't drown a duck."

They forfeited, and we kept his words as our motto.

Mom even used us as an example at a town meeting when we were about to lose our school band.

"We're up to our ears in taxes!" someone ranted. "Something's got to go, we're drowning here!"

"You can't drown a duck, Mr. Sanders," Mom said. "And aren't we all Ducks here in Riverton?" She was a rousing speaker. "I'd like to hear how the rest of you feel about this—"

My dad was on his feet. "Keep the band! Go, Ducks!"

A young father handed his baby to his wife and also jumped up. "Go, Ducks!"

Then the whole hall was chanting, "Go, Ducks! Go, Ducks! Go, Ducks!"

When they quieted down, Mom said, "You can't drown a Duck—not with water and not with taxes—one dime apiece will keep our band and our spirits alive in Riverton!"

When the citizens stopped clapping, the majority voted to pay their dime.

That's what I mean by Ducks, and by Riverton spirit.

o o o

I wasn't exactly the star of the Ducks, but I sometimes played a little of the first game, and definitely almost always played in the second. Since the season was over, we practiced inside the gym, four afternoons and one morning a week. We were very exciting to watch—like a roomful of spirited squirrels.

Afternoon practices always had a rousing crowd of moms,

but my mom couldn't come because of work, and Dad had after-noon phone conferences.

"Mom, I'm the only one with no one!"

"No you aren't, Birdie. And I never miss a real game. Plus your dad gets up at six in the morning so he can go on Thursdays. Right?"

"Dad does. You don't."

We'd have a sighing contest.

It was true Dad was the star parent for Thursday before-school drills. In fact he was usually the only one who made it.

Our team name was of course the Ducks, but when we divided for drills, half of us were called Feathers and half were called Beaks.

I was a Beak, which I hated on account of my large-nose fear.

Meredith, who's just a totally awesome goalie, was a Feather. When I actually got the ball past her one morning, Dad should have yelled, "Go, Beaks!"

"Go, Ducks," he said.

"*Beaks,* Dad!" I yelled to him. He sat smack in the middle of the bleachers, nose large enough to refract light.

I rounded the gym, feet flailing, and went for the goal again.

"Go, Beaks," Dad said.

"Not yet, Dad!"

I kicked the hide off that ball, but Meredith caught it, slammed it clear back to the other side of the gym.

"Go, Ducks."

I knew it was Meredith that Dad was cheering for this time;

he knew all the girls and made it clear from the start he was for everyone.

"*Feathers,* Dad—" I yelled breathlessly. "Meredith is a *Feather!*"

It's a hard job, being in charge of the cheers as well as playing. I passed the ball to Samantha and sat heavily on the bench. The coach was smiling at the floor. "Good job, Sidwell."

"Thanks, Coach!"

o o o

Dad had gotten back from Washington, D.C., while I was at school. It had been an amazing trip. The Department of Agriculture had specially shipped in a batch of Dad's latest wonder beans, and Dad got to personally present them to the president of a drought-stricken African country. It was a big moment for Dad. His plan was actually beginning to work! Mom and I were so proud of him.

They both picked me up from school and I hugged Dad about twelve times. Mom suggested we celebrate his success with cocoa. Even in May, the river can cast a cold blue chill down the streets of Riverton. We snugged our table close to the kitchen fireplace and I lit an instant log.

The light flickered warmly. Hot mugs of cocoa sat in front of us. We began doing the things we do: Dad hunched over his laptop, typing out a report for Washington; Mom sorted through the mail; I stared at the flames while a story circled my brain, possible endings nipping at it like sheepdogs.

I hauled out the special journal my parents had given me. It had a soft leather cover that said BIRDIE'S PRIVATE JOURNAL, and hundreds of pages for my original stories and word lists and private thoughts. A satin ribbon marked my place.

I uncapped my pen and began: "Isabella would never have drowned if only she'd listened to her piano teacher—"

Suddenly Mom snatched a large official-looking envelope from the pile and held it up to us.

Our passports!

She inspected each one carefully. I tugged on her sleeve, bugging her to see mine, wondering aloud how many bathing suits I'd be needing and when we could go to Portland to shop.

"When *can* we, Mom? It's only three weeks. It's got to be Lloyd's Center—I need a *lot* of stuff. I need a *list*—"

She smiled and handed me my passport, a royal-feeling little book just about me.

"Yes," she said. "We all need lists, and it's certainly not too soon to start packing and closing up the house. Henry? I'm hoping you'll be in charge of that."

Dad blinked at his passport sitting there in front of him. "So," he said. "The trip is upon us."

"*Birdwinkle!*" I cried, staring at the name under my passport picture. I flapped it at Mom. "How could you let them use that, Mom? I hate *Birdwinkle;* now all the people on St. Petts will be calling me that!"

"And I hate it when you yell and we're all sitting right here beside you." Her words were quiet but sharp-edged as stop signs.

I lowered my passport, accidentally dipping one edge into my cocoa.

She sighed. "This is a government document, Birdie. They don't use nicknames on government documents—"

Dad broke in. "And, Birdie! I don't believe you mean to say you hate *Birdwinkle,* without him we'd be—"

"I don't hate Bivens Birdwinkle, Dad." I stared at the soggy corner of my passport, knowing without asking that I wouldn't be getting a new one. "I just wish you'd considered it a little more when you named your only daughter after him."

"Oh, I *did,* Birdie, in fact I pondered the issue for months—"

Mom gathered our passports and fanned them like a winning hand of cards. Dad and I fell silent.

She said, "Just look! Passports to paradise for one entire year! No wonder we're a little excitable."

"A year, Clara?" Dad's pale skin went paler. "Is that really what we decided?"

"Yes, Henry." Stop signs again. "It is."

I looked at Dad. Dad looked at Mom.

He cleared his throat. "Well then, I'm looking forward to it, Clara." He smiled his crookedy smile. "Maybe I'll even farm a little while we're there, grow a few beans!"

Mom said, "Perfect, Henry. You can grow beans on St. Petts! Just what the Caribbean is famous for, *beans.*"

She raised her cup and Dad and I clinked it.

I don't know why we all laughed so long. I guess we were just beside ourselves.

chapter
6

morgan

As was so often the case, the beauty of the rising sun caught me by surprise. I sat beneath sails rearing like unruly white stallions and was astonished by the new day.

Heaped around me on the deck were snippets of hair. I lowered a huge pair of scissors and systematically pulled at the remaining hanks on my head, checking to see if they were more or less the same length.

The feel of cropped hair was good. It reminded me of happy days. Always, when I was small and we had set freshly out to sea, Oona would cut our hair, Mother nodding approval.

There was no one to nod now, but the feeling remained.

I swept the deck, adjusted the sails, and was surprised to find I was not alone: Another vessel moved in from the horizon. I was far enough out at sea that the sight of another ship was rare. The big ships, cargo ships that can be city blocks in length, city buildings in height, must be well avoided, as they cannot easily change their path. More often I passed boats similar in size to my own, either power- or sailboats. Some of them, the grand yachts, are even more completely outfitted for world navigation than mine, and far more opulently furnished.

This morning I saw a sleek black-hulled sailboat, elaborately rigged with expensive radar. I picked up the binoculars but could not make out its name.

My sailboat is the *Svanhild*, Norwegian for *swan*. My parents had her specially built for them, which gave them the right to name her. She is white up and down, black masts and rigging, and in every way as powerful and graceful as a swan.

The black yacht was powerful as well, but with larger sails, arranged differently. It approached rapidly to starboard—my right. It is customary to contact ships within sight, to verify your presence and avoid collision. It is also an opportunity for chat, if you are a traveler who enjoys chat. I don't care for chat, but I do obey the laws of courtesy and safety.

I glanced at the compass, set the sails to pilot the boat without me, and swung down the steps of the companionway to the interior. My navigation station was right there, handily positioned for checking charts and for using the radio and radar and satellite equipment.

"Black-hulled yacht, black-hulled yacht," I said into the speaker. "Clipper *Svanhild* to your port side." I released the call button of the speaker and waited.

An elderly voice with a German accent said, "*Svanhild, Svanhild, Engelberta* has you in sight. Over and out."

Engelberta. The Bright Angel. I smiled. Our boats were our prides.

"Over and out, *Engelberta.*"

I nodded. I imagined the elderly German captain did as well. An efficient exchange requiring nothing more.

I returned to deck and watched the *Engelberta* sail by.

It came close enough that I could see the brass gleam of the winches, the golden lacquered wood, a radar system such as I had never seen before. It appeared nearly new. A sweet-faced elderly woman, gray hair pinned up in braids, waved slowly. Perhaps the captain's original bright angel. I raised a hand in return.

The *Engelberta* was uncommonly fast, and my sailboat wallowed in its wake.

When it had become a small mark on the opposite horizon, I pulled off my shirt and completed my morning grooming, soaping my face, my hard-muscled arms and lean stomach, rinsing with a precious bowlful of fresh water. Careful toothbrushing followed: Neglected teeth can cause great trouble at sea. Then I urinated in a bucket used only for that, rinsing it in seawater once the contents had been tossed overboard.

I ate two oranges, a luxury from land. As Mother had taught me, I wasted nothing, chewing even the seeds and swallowing them.

Most hours, I prefer silence to sound. The exception is that each morning when I scrub the salty topside of the boat, I turn on the radio to receive music from Jamaica. Reggae empties troubling thoughts from my mind, and keeps my motions loose and rhythmic.

This morning, the popular musician Dreadful Calabash sang out, his tune spilling over the deck and bumping across the empty sea. In the background, I heard steel drums, and Oona's voice. She was always a fancier of jump-ups.

I smiled and leaped to my feet to join them. My body spun and my head wheeled this way and that on my neck. I sprang repeatedly to smack my soap brush against the boom that swung eight feet over the deck. The lather spattered the brass portholes and my face and legs, but these were things I could easily wipe clean. Once I returned again to my normal world of silence.

chapter

Birdie

My going-away party was extremely lively.

It was the principal, Mr. Levison's, idea that there be a special send-off for me and my family at the Cloud Dance—held the last Friday night of every school year. Of course, leave it to Mrs. Kimball to get right in the middle of everything! Her husband was never in town and she didn't work, so she had a lot of time to *be involved*.

A week before the dance, I was just leaving school when she rushed up to me.

"Oh, Birdie, how exciting for you, the Caribbean for a whole year, however does your mother do it on her salary."

"Dad works too, Mrs. Kimball. He's a genius, you know."

"Do tell. What are they paying geniuses today?"

"A lot, Mrs. Kimball."

"Well, won't Kirin be missing you. I have big news for her, too. I'm saving it until the night of the Cloud Dance, isn't that nice?"

"As long as you don't throw a pot of flowers at my head it is."

Did I say that? I'd never been anything but polite to Mrs.

Kimball! I certainly had never spoken of what she'd done that day at the sandbox!

"What are you talking about, Birdie Sidwell?" She actually raised her little square purse like she was going to hit me on the head with it. "When did you get so smart-alecky, anyway? Clara ought to be sending you to Nu-Way, not some tropical island where everyone runs around half-dressed and devil-may-care and you'll only get more the way you already are—"

She took a deep breath. Her temper always caught her by surprise. "Well, goodness, what are we fussing for, and here it is the last week of school." She smoothed the side of her purse as though calming a dog that had almost bitten someone. "I just wanted to say I'm in charge of food and decoration for the dance and I've chosen Caribbean Splendors as the theme. You have to dress in costume to get in, something sunny yet modest. Be sure to tell your father, he always wears the same clothes—"

"They're not the *same clothes*, Mrs. Kimball. He has a lot of clothes that happen to be similar—"

Her eyes swiveled to the school door. Mr. Wynn was pushing out. As always, he was surrounded by kids. He was dressed in black, muscles showing through his T-shirt, spiky hair just perfect. I saw her strain to keep her attack purse under control. "Sweet Jesus! I mean, good grief! Is that the new music teacher? Dressed like that? What about the dress code? Rules are rules!"

Like no cats in her yard? I wanted to say, *There's no rule about black T-shirts, Mrs. Kimball,* but I was just too chicken.

She frowned. "To finish what I was saying, I chose

Caribbean Splendors because the Cloud Dance is apparently all about you this year. . . . That you're leaving us . . ."

Our eyes actually met for a moment, taking in the fact of it. Then we cast our eyes down, studied the sidewalk.

She said quietly, "We will miss you, Birdie. Truly."

For every ten nasty things Mrs. Kimball says, she says one thing nice, making me forget all over again who she is.

"Thank you, Mrs. Kimball. And thank you for the Caribbean Splendors theme. Sorry if I was rude."

"Well. Sorry I said 'half-dressed,' that wasn't very nice, was it? Oh, here he comes—what's his name? Mr. Wynn?" She plucked at his arm as he passed. "Mr. Wynn, are you going to be the disk jockey at the Cloud Dance? I want to be sure my decor and your tunes match up."

In the misty light, the dyed-green tips of his blond crew cut gave off a particularly alien glow.

He said, "O sure t'ing, mon," using a perfect Jamaican accent. He was the coolest teacher at middle school! "I be bring d'Wailers, d'Dreadful Calabash, jam all day, jump-up all d'night."

He did a little calypso step and Mrs. Kimball frowned. "I didn't understand one word of that except *calabash.*" He offered no translation. She tried again. "Do you mean you're playing tunes about *fruit?*"

The kids tittered, then drifted off into small groups.

"Tunes d'be from Mangoland, where everybody happy."

"Mangos," she muttered, headed for her car. "And calabash. Is that a fruit or a vegetable? Oh well, it's a start—"

I imagined her doing something gross like roasting a pig with an apple in its mouth. That would be so like her.

I said, "I'm glad you're doing reggae, Mr. Wynn. My mom's a huge fan of Bob Marley. She dances like a . . . a . . . flying geranium when she hears his music."

"Who doesn't!" He waved his arms flying geranium-style. "And aren't you just the luckiest duck, going off to an island?"

"I am!" I cried. "Go, Ducks!"

I did a perfect cartwheel right there in front of school. School might be out, but my school spirit was a lifelong thing.

o o o

Instead of going straight home, I went to Opal's Finery, looking for an outfit for my party. I usually wear greens and teals to show off my red hair, but my eyes immediately picked out a bright orange-patterned halter and long scarf displayed with the bathing suits.

In the dressing room I wrapped the scarf low over my bare hips, raised my arms, and rotated my stomach in slow sexy circles. I felt just like that singer Courtney Starz! But when I looked in the mirror, a curly-haired kid frowned back, ribs flaring in and out as she bucked around the tiny room. It was a little discouraging.

I sighed my mother's sigh and hitched the scarf into normal skirt position. That wasn't so bad. And my chest was definitely making progress. The halter fit fine—

A sharp voice broke from the next dressing room: "I *hate* it, I told you already!"

"Well, you're not wearing a bathing suit to a dance, I can tell you that much—"

Kirin and her mom. I thought the years of Nu-Way had put an end to their bickering.

"Quit it, Mom! I'm not putting it on!"

"Fine, but I'm buying it, and you're wearing it. I can't think of anything more Caribbean-splendid than a muumuu."

"It's *hideous*!"

"You have totally reverted without Mr. Nudleman! What would your dad say if he heard you?"

"Dad never hears me because Dad's never home, Mother dear! Because Dad can't *stand* you and neither can I—"

There was a crash and a whimper. Had Mrs. Kimball hit her? I know she used to. How did Kirin get the nerve to stand up to her? I knew too well how Mrs. Kimball could switch in an instant, from sweet-voiced mother to raging maniac. The crashing started up again, this time like they were wrestling each other!

I heard Miss Opal, her frail little voice worried on the other side of the curtain. "Mrs. Kimball? Everything all right? It's too crowded in there, isn't it? For two?"

Mrs. Kimball's voice was high and short of breath. "Oh no, we're fine in here, Opal! Just a tiny bit tight."

She spoke a few low words to Kirin, and Kirin said in a bright Nu-Way tone of voice, "We're perfectly fine. It's an opportunity for getting close!"

I looked in the mirror again, my face so tense and sad I hardly recognized myself.

This is how it was for poor Kirin! Caught between a fake world at home and her own faked personality. For a moment I stood lost in awe at how she'd kept her spirit. Endured years of her mother and Mr. Nudleman. Her captors. No wonder she was so mean to me; I was the only one she was safe enough with to let it out!

I sighed. Well, at least she didn't have to go to Nu-Way anymore. I grabbed my new outfit and sneaked to the register. The last thing I wanted to do was pretend to the Kimballs that I hadn't heard what I'd heard.

o o o

I had a very long bath the afternoon of the party, soaked myself in Mom's Tropical Passion, then leisurely used up my inspired phrases in an essay about how my new life would go. I did one scene each on:

1. Our rented bungalow.

2. The people of St. Petts.

3. How I imagined them gathering on our beach each sunset to watch my American cartwheels.

Mom and I spent some time admiring each other in our new outfits. We looked tan and cute because we'd started faux-tanning the instant our airline tickets had arrived. She was wearing her prized new dress, a silky blue caftan with dolphins leaping around its hem.

My own halter top and flowing skirt were bright as the sun. With the tan, I felt confident enough to show a little tummy. And I'd put on makeup: glittery blush, shell-pink lip gloss, sea-blue eye shadow. Even the mirror was impressed!

We rubbed instant tanning lotion all over Dad's face and arms and legs, which wasn't easy because he's really, really ticklish. When he came downstairs a little later, wearing baggy shorts, a Hawaiian shirt, and a straw hat, we hardly knew him.

"Dad, you're so *cute*!"

"You *are*, Henry—and you look so . . . *healthy*!"

With the hat covering up his mostly bald head, he definitely looked younger and . . . cuter.

Mom slipped sunglasses on him, then leaned forward to kiss his nose.

He smiled, and they gazed at each other the way they do.

Mom put on a Dreadful Calabash CD, and we danced around Dad like he was our sun god. I noticed again how great Mom was looking, slimmed down, eyes shiny with anticipation.

"You're like Cher or someone, Mom—like Madonna! A real sexy older person."

Dad nodded and she smiled at both of us, her adoring family.

I put on my slicker, which didn't begin to cover my fake-tan legs, and we stepped into the rain.

"Hope my legs don't run."

Dad said, "Hope they do! Race you!"

We ran all the way to school, slickers flapping noisily inside the quiet night fog, a ridiculous sight even to ourselves. Then we were inside the gym, breathless, joining all the important people of our lives.

We looked up and for a moment, there was a catch in our smiles. The banner read:

GOODBYE, BIRDIE!

Mr. Wynn was *on* the music! Kids, seniors, toddlers flung themselves around the huge room, everyone showing off their bright Caribbean costumes. The entire town seemed to be there except Kirin, who was no doubt waiting to make her grand entrance.

The gym dripped with plastic fruit: bananas, oranges, and papayas. Calabash rattles hung from the center of the ceiling like a prized chandelier, and a yellow happy-face sun shone down on the Caribbean Splendors.

Mrs. Kimball moved briskly in and out of the center of things. Her long frilly white apron worn over a full-skirted mango-colored dress made her look dressed for church—or a fifties sitcom. Still, she kept interesting food coming from the cafeteria: coconut goodies, little vegetable fritters, nothing like roast pig in sight. I felt a little ashamed of always thinking the worst of her.

She handed me a paper cup of punch.

"Welcome to the Cloud Dance, Birdie. A humble *bon voyage* from Riverton to the Sidwells." Speaking as though she were the town representative. She lowered her voice and leaned closer. "Kirin and I are going to be doing some traveling of our own. Nothing like your family of course, so extravagant, but a nice trip up the coast. She doesn't even know yet—it's our little secret."

"Nice, Mrs. Kimball. Clear to Seattle?"

She nodded.

Seattle shopping was way cooler than Portland shopping. "Kirin'll be in heaven!"

Mrs. Kimball had on her lipstick smile, something I could never read.

I was relieved that the two of them had made up and were doing something fun together.

I danced two dances with Max, who was a pretty nice guy when he wasn't busy being a football hero. Through the buzz of the crowd, I heard Mr. Wynn say to someone, "I'm going up now; it's time to bring on Birdie."

Max heard it too, looked down at me, and gave me a friendly little shove. My heart raced in anticipation of what would happen next. I'd never been a celebrity! We watched Mr. Wynn work his way toward a platform that looked like the home of Chiquita Banana. He dragged the mike onstage. It screeched on. My stomach felt like a cocoon about to hatch a million butterflies.

This was my moment—

He opened his mouth to speak, but the amplified words that came out were not his. It wasn't even a man's voice!

"Hi, evr'one."

Every head swiveled to the stage. It was Kirin, draped in a flowered red plus-sized muumuu, plastic lei hanging crookedly from her perfect pale swan neck!

She lurched around Mr. Wynn, took the mike, and like a born thief, she stole my moment.

"Is me, Kir'n Kimball."

Mr. Wynn's jaw snapped closed. I could see his struggle to make sense of things. He gave a little bow and stepped away from the mike.

She leaned too close to it and her words broke over the gym like water balloons.

"'Sa big cel'bration, huh." She tottered and grabbed for the stand.

"She's *drunk*!" Max said.

Mr. Wynn reached for the mike but she had it.

"Jess want to say, bye, old friend Birdie." She peered into the gym and tried to focus on me. "Bye-bye, Birdie."

I winced. Even drunk, she just had to say that.

She gave a weak wave, shielded her eyes, and squinted back into the audience. "And Mother dear?"

Mr. Wynn took her arm. "Kirin—"

"*Uh*-uh!" Kirin pulled sharply away, scowled at him.

"Mr. Levison?" he called, motioning across the gym for the principal.

Kirin breathed into the mike. "Jess wanted to say I'm a g'girl, Mother, look, all dressed up Cribian for you—"

Mrs. Kimball was slicing her way through the stunned crowd like a serrated knife.

For a drunk person, Kirin's next move was surprisingly swift. Her muumuu was suddenly lying on the stage floor like a squeezed-dry tomato. Kirin stood next to it in nothing but a string bikini.

"Splendors, Mother," Kirin said, glancing down at herself. "Looky here."

There was no one *not* looking.

They were the smallest bikini, the highest heels, ever worn inside the Riverton city limits. The bikini was the exact tawny pink of Kirin's own skin: The more you stared at her the nakeder she looked.

I just couldn't believe what I was seeing! She was usually very modest. I don't think I'd ever seen her this undressed, even in the locker room! She clutched the mike stand to steady the wobble of her heels. Under the unfamiliar makeup, she looked sick and scared.

I managed to tear my eyes away from her extremely grown-up body long enough to see Mrs. Kimball charge up the stage steps. She unwrapped her apron as she strode to her daughter.

"Hello, Mother dear."

Mrs. Kimball's broad face twisted to the side. She jerked her daughter's arm and in one move, pivoted her inside the big apron and tied it with an immense bow.

Mr. Levison was suddenly there, he and Mr. Wynn reaching for Kirin. Mrs. Kimball pushed her into their arms.

She spoke into the mike. "Thank you, gentlemen, for assisting my daughter, who's suffering the side effects of her allergy medication. Poor thing!"

She raised her hands to applaud her daughter, nodded to

the audience that they should join in. A few confused claps followed, petered out.

Inside the billow of white apron, a captured swan again,
Kirin let the men lead her away. Her footsteps clacked as loudly
down the steps as they had that terrible day when she was taken
from second grade.

Run, I wanted to say, *fly away.*

As if she heard me, she slipped from their grasp and darted
into the crowd. Mr. Wynn looked at Mr. Levison. They both
shrugged and looked up at Mrs. Kimball. It was the mother who
should take over, that seemed obvious enough.

"Jeez," Max said, having trouble with what he'd seen. "Kirin's
drunk and she's *naked. . . .*"

"Get a grip, Max," I said. "She has a hard life."

"She does?"

Was he stupid? How had he not noticed? How had any of us
not noticed—

"Dear friends of Riverton," Mrs. Kimball's voice boomed
out. Leave it to her to feel she had to make a speech at a time like
this! "Could the evening be lovelier?"

My special evening had been about as lovely as a trip to the
dentist! It occurred to me for the first time that Mrs. Kimball
might actually be insane. I saw my parents standing under a
bright light near the refreshment table. Their shocked eyes told
me they were thinking the same thing.

Mrs. Kimball's words were rushed, her eyes cutting to Kirin
as she made her way toward Max. "We're all here to say goodbye,
temporarily goodbye—at least unless they never come back—

to our superintendent of schools, Clara Sidwell, and her husband, Henry Sidwell, and most especially to our small friend Birdie Sidwell."

Everyone cheered.

But what about that never coming back part? No one had ever suggested *that* before! Just Mrs. Kimball's way, I guessed. Hateful to the end.

I smiled at my friends, friends I would miss every single day I was gone! And then Kirin was pushing her way past Max, reaching for me.

"Goodbye, Sidwells," Mrs. Kimball said abruptly, and left the mike swaying on its stand as she bolted after her daughter.

Mr. Levison strode toward the microphone, his smile stretched thin.

"Kirin!" Mrs. Kimball's voice was small beneath the reassuring drone of the principal's words, but Kirin heard it. Her head swiveled, eyes suddenly alert.

Then Mrs. Kimball had her by the arm.

"Okay, Kirin, this isn't how I wanted to tell you." Her voice was furious. "But now you've done it. It was supposed to be a surprise; Birdie knows all about it—"

Kirin looked at me, eyes filled with silent questions.

I shrugged, tried to smile encouragingly.

Mrs. Kimball said, "I've enrolled you at the Nu-Way up in Seattle. Year-round. You've left me no choice. Mr. Nudleman and I agree *you must be returned to the flock.*"

That stupid flock thing again! Only now Kirin would be *living* there!

Mrs. Kimball was positively twitching inside her flouncy dress. "This school has *ruined* you, Kirin. Just look at yourself—"

Kirin looked down at the frenzied wrap of white apron, her shapely arms and legs hanging out.

"I'm driving you up there in one week—"

"Mom! No!" Her eyes filled with tears. "Birdie, you *knew*?"

"Wow," said Max, shaking his head at me. "You knew?" As if he had anything to do with anything!

I hadn't even realized my parents had moved to stand close behind me until Dad put a protective hand on my shoulder.

Mrs. Kimball's voice was suddenly loud and cheerful. "Anyway!" she said. "Congratulations, my darling, you're off to Nu-Way again." She glanced at my parents and then planted a kiss on her daughter's pale cheek. "There's nothing more to say."

Kirin glared at me as though it were all my fault.

"This was bound to happen!" she cried out.

I had no idea what she meant by that. I reached for her, wanting to tell her I hadn't known it was coming. To tell her . . . I don't know what.

But she broke free of our circle and fled from the gym.

My parents were scandalized by the harsh turn of the evening. They drew me close, as if Mr. Nudleman skulked in the shadowy corners of the gym, ready to leap from behind plastic palm fronds with his child-stealing net.

The speeches were over, the music back on, but not even Mr. Wynn could come up with enough cheer to save the party after that.

o o o

My parents didn't make a big thing about it, the bikini or the Nu-Way announcement. *Poor Kirin,* is what we were all thinking, but we were too busy with the last-minute details of our own life to figure out what was going on with the Kimballs.

The night before we left, I'd officially snapped my main trunk closed, and now I was just finishing up my extra suitcase. I wore bathing suits under my clothes all the time now, breaking them in, feeling their springy newness and imagining how their colors would come alive once I was in the ocean, wearing my snorkeling mask. Which I also wore around the house quite a bit. I couldn't see much through it and it left some nasty red marks around my mouth, but wearing it excited my imagination almost as much as a bath.

I had it on and was sitting on my bed after dinner, writing a story about being captured by Caribbean pirates, when Kirin climbed in my window. I was flabbergasted. She hadn't done anything like that since she was seven! It was an easy climb, but still! We didn't just go into each other's rooms like that anymore!

I peeled off the snorkel mask and she sat carefully by my side, not even looking at me. Her face was completely empty, like someone had turned her upside down and spilled her personality into the ground.

She began speaking in a flat voice. "I'm sorry I've been mean to you, Birdie. I'm a mean person, I guess . . . like Mother. It's just you have everything—"

"I don't have *every*thing, Keers. I didn't even get an orange Mac for my birthday I got a plain PC—"

"That's what I mean, it's so easy for you, all in the world you want is an orange Mac!" She shook her head. "I barely have *myself* anymore. Anything that's left of me, Mother's trying to Nudelize. . . . You don't know how hard it is, hanging on to who I really am. Sometimes I can hardly remember. The teachers act so nice until you don't do what they want and then they embarrass you to death. When that happens, I try to remember that time we were little kids . . . ?"

I nodded. We never talked about it, but "that time" must have been even scarier for her. After all, it was her mother who threw the flowerpot that could have killed us.

She said, "You got so sick; I mean you've been kind of sick ever since—"

"Kirin! I'm *not* sick anymore. I'm catching up, haven't you seen that?"

"Umm. Sorry, Birdie, I do see that. That's what I mean, I say brutal stuff, just like my mother. But, that time? . . . You were so brave. I remember looking at you in the hospital—that's when it started with us, wasn't it?" I nodded again. "You never blamed anybody or even told what Mother did; you just kept on going. The way I stay brave is by pretending I'm you, Birdie. I'm just trying to keep on going. . . ."

She started to cry very softly. I reached to hold her.

It was almost a shock, hugging her again after so many hands-off years. Her hair smelled good, the same herbal shampoo as always. I was flooded with memories of combing each other's hair as children, combing and braiding each other's hair for hours. . . .

"Kirin! Why don't you come with us? I'll put you in my trunk instead of clothes; we'll write your mother from St. Petts. . . ."

She smiled through her tears. "Oh, Birdie, only you'd think of that." She shook her head. "I can't. But don't worry—I'm not giving in."

"You can't drown a Duck."

We both laughed, if that's what you can call those blubbery sounds.

She said, "I just came by to tell you I wish I'd been a better friend, and now you're leaving—and I'm leaving."

"Goodbye, Kirin." Sounds broke from me that neither of us tried to pretend were laughter. "You're still my friend."

"Goodbye, Birdie. You're mine, too."

She climbed out the window and once more was gone from my life.

o o o

Mom found me there with my snorkel mask back in place, writing in my journal, crying so hard I was completely fogged in and nearly drowning.

Actually, now that my tears for Kirin had passed, I was enjoying the experience. In my imagination, I was deep underwater, looking up at the dark hull of a boat, crying my heart out at seeing that I'd been daggered and that my death was near at hand.

"A heinous ending to my young life," I scribbled. *"An ending both preposterous and—"*

"Birdie?" Mom was standing over me, smoothing my tangled curls. "Having a last-minute meltdown?" She removed my snotty mask and looked into bleary eyes. "No wonder, sweetie. What we're doing is huge, so many changes . . ."

We smiled at each other.

She said, "Maybe you shouldn't wear that mask all the time. You're really getting some grooves in your poor face."

"Okay." I sniffed. "Why do you think Nudleman started those schools?"

"I don't have a clue, honey. Have you been dwelling on Nu-Way? On poor Kirin?" She was quiet for a moment. "Unfortunately Mrs. Kimball has turned into one of those mothers to be overcome. But Kirin could turn out to be a very strong person because of all this."

"She is strong, Mom. She'll never let herself get Nudelized."

Mom raised her eyebrows at the phrase, but for a change, I didn't say anything more.

She sighed, then turned her head to frown at the heaps of things that weren't going to make it into my suitcase.

I got the point, sighing back as I started to pick up the floor, fold clothes, get my poor room ready for a year without me there to cheer it up.

"We leave for Portland at five in the morning," she reminded me. "Finish up now, hop in bed . . . no more stories for tonight, okay? No more thoughts about Nudleman. There will always be people like Nudleman out there, bullying others."

"Okay, Mom. Good night."

"'Night, honey."

chapter 8

MORGAN

Twilight brings no more danger than any other hour at sea. But it is the time of greatest anxiety for me. My parents had been unaware of me for so long, I was sure I knew the feeling of traveling alone into the night. But it's been four days now, and three nights, and I see I was wrong. Without them, my boat feels hollow, and the new silence is even harsher than the old.

But they were no longer fit to sail, and I will never be more so. It is the way of things.

The surface of this evening's sea was calm but greatly inflated. We were gently buoyed above water canyons, slipped down into their dark hollows, brought up again into the fading light. By morning my sailboat would be fighting a chaotic sea, the wheel hard and scraping in my hands. Storm on the way: something I knew. The other, the ship being mine alone, was something I did not know.

Oona?

Oona, are we all right?

The sea is always right.

But what about finding others? Like myself? I'm alone.

If solitude is not right for you, seek others.

I nodded. Oona always had answers, even if they weren't quite what I'd asked for.

In some ways, it is as if all comprehensible events took place before I turned nine. I did not clearly understand what happened to Oona when she disappeared into the sea; that she would be gone forever. Without her to explain, how could I know? She was the only one of my family who spoke to me beyond practical matters.

With her, all work was play: navigating, tying knots, calling dolphins, marching into the jungles with satchels of rice for the hungry. I saw now that those times of play would have to last me the rest of my life. Oona's voice remained, but the comfort of sleeping, playing, bathing with another child was gone.

Perhaps my best moment with Oona, at least the time I most recall, happened not long before she went to live inside the sea:

She was twelve and I was nine. I had been noticing a new precociousness in her. Even at her young age, she was being drawn to boys. Boys noticed her as well, when she sought them out onshore, wanting to know the mystery of their boyhood. She wanted this with the same intensity with which I did *not* want it.

Her way of challenging boys, of provoking them, did not seem a satisfactory kind of play to me. But perhaps to them it was.

One memorable day we were far at sea, an unusually calm sea. We had tied up to a ramshackle boat, a large family adrift on their stalled fishing vessel. By the greatest good fortune, Father saw their fishing pole raised with a tattered cloth and came to the rescue. He had the parts required to repair their engine, and Mother had the ability to do it. We would be tied up for an entire day for her to complete the job.

The children of course gathered as far from the parents as possible, on the deck of the *Svanhild*. Enrico, the eldest son, was an older boy with a dark feathering above his upper lip and black hair that grew in quills. He and Oona circled each other like cats.

Oona dared anything. She said, "I can hold my breath longer than anyone."

"Uh-uh," he said, smiling, liking that she'd said this. "You can't."

"I can go into the sea and do it longer than you."

The younger children, me included, were scandalized by speaking of going into the sea. The most forbidden of things.

Enrico said, "Uh-uh," but I could see he was willing to follow this wherever it went.

Oona pulled off her shirt.

Enrico said, "Tsss," and pulled off his own.

They dropped a rope and climbed silently into the water, careful not to draw the attention of the parents. I could see Oona repeatedly filling her lungs with oxygen as she descended. When she went under, she already had the advantage. They dived from the surface, Oona a sea otter, Enrico a retriever pup.

I began counting, and the other children softly joined in. At 139, Enrico was back, gasping, shaking the water from his eyes, looking for Oona.

Oona rose to the surface at 232. It was her best by seventeen counts.

Enrico smiled at her and shook his head. "Uh-uh."

They studied each other for a minute, Oona's long eyes suddenly dreamy. She pulled him underwater with her for so long, the rest of us became bored and drifted over to the helm to eat a sack of oranges.

Enrico came up the rope alone and disappeared onto the fishing boat.

"Morgan!" whispered Oona. "Come down with me."

I was instantly down, pushing into the cool buoyancy with her.

"I made him kiss me," she said. "He was afraid."

"Umm," I said. My eyes popped at her boldness, and more than that, her creativity.

And then, heedless of getting discovered by Father, we played in the water. I, too, could hold my breath well. We dived deeper and deeper, searching the navy-blue murk for dolphins. Oona had always told me dolphins were our brothers and sisters; she gestured now that we should call for them with the saved-up air in our lungs.

We did, but no sister or brother dolphins came. It didn't matter. What I remember is the feel of Oona, hauling me this way and that under the water, challenging me but never making me afraid. The pleasure of tumbling in the water with Oona is what has stayed with me, and what I most wish for when I am lonely.

O O O

It was time to check the charts, to decide at which port to provision. I had not wanted to alarm my parents with needless announcements of my departure and so had done nothing to stock the boat for travel.

By now, they would know everything. They had been on their own for four days. The worst would be over: returning late that first night, drunken and silly. An empty slip waiting instead of their boat. That would have been the worst of it, but still merely awkward and without danger. Perhaps Father would have had a moment of concern over me. Mother would know I was all right—*tough as a little squid* is what she always said of me.

They would find a new dwelling without trouble. Something near the marina and their fellow rum drinkers. A place where they could hear and see and smell their sea, without losing their lives for the privilege.

I'd left a parcel for them with the harbormaster: papers, numbers of one of our adequate money accounts, the leather satchel filled with their sturdy, well-worn clothes. There were no keepsakes to gather beyond a few early photos of themselves. They'd kept nothing along the way to remind them of their lives at sea, or the two children they had lost there.

Oona? Why was it you fell? Was it your fault—that you couldn't hold on? Or Mother's fault, to let you be there?

It was bound to happen.

I frowned.

After the baby, Mother used the rum to try to fix her heart. After Oona, Father joined in. It never fixed them. It ruined their minds and their bodies.

Before I was thirteen years old, I had taken their place as captain. I repaired the boat, charted our course, purchased a new computer to manage the money accumulated from Father's working days. Money that grew on its own and was always there for fuel and new canvas and vegetables when we were lucky enough to find them.

After Oona, my parents sought land for drink rather than work.

"Morgan, we must go ashore." Mother would rise blinking from the dark interior of the boat, squint at me through the sunshine.

"A small harbor," she said, watching me at the helm, watching for oversteering. "Small but with stores."

Rum stores.

Her long, storm-broken face searched my eyes for signs of defiance. Oona had defiance, but I did not.

"Yes, Mother. We can be in Dominica in four days."

"Three—three days at most."

"That would be Martinique." We never went to Martinique to provision. Too expensive.

She glanced sideways: Would I say it? *Too expensive?*

I did not say it; it was she who emphasized thrift. But I did not look away.

Who was in charge, mother or daughter?

The question hung there in the air, neither of us caring to look at it.

Of course we would go to Martinique—we had the money—but what if I had said, "I choose not to, Mother. I have thought about it and it's too expensive. Your rum habit will have to wait another day."

Would she have nodded and said, "You have chosen right, and now it is you who shall be in charge."

Or would she have said, "You will have to leave if you do not obey your mother. I have lost two children, what is one more?"

I was too young. I had none of the words and none of the defiance. If I had hoped—and none of us were hopeful children—I might have hoped not to make hard choices at all.

So I said nothing, and Mother went below again to be with her bottles instead of with her daughter.

But now I was seventeen, with no one aboard to keep me from choosing freely.

I'd left my parents in Panama. They'd planned to sail through the canal and enter another ocean, the Pacific Ocean. I thought it a bad idea. None of us had experience with that sea, a fierce sea despite its gentle name. My parents were no longer able to take on such challenges.

I returned instead to the heart of the Caribbean sea, the sea where I was born.

Should I now head south to Venezuela? Always cheap canned goods, although the waters near Caracas were hectic with traffic. And once there, the harbor officials were unpredictable, changing the rules and the fees according to the look of your pocketbook.

Or I could go north to Puerto Rico. A fine long voyage ending with familiar, lighthearted ports and an excellent selection of spare engine parts and hardware.

Oona?

All ports offer companionship.

Canned goods, Oona. What is best for that?

All ports offer canned goods.

All right. I choose Venezuela. I would check the charts; several years ago we'd provisioned in a small town up one of the rivers past Caracas. El Gordito, a flat dry place that featured one single, perfectly round hill.

I adjusted the sails and the autopilot for an hour of self-sailing, then plotted my course below and returned to deck to stand night watch. My numbers were calculated on paper and in the computer, but I gauged the wind and the sea by feel. This is the way of a born sailor.

My father had said, "I am a learned sailor, but you and Oona are born to the sea. It is the same to you as it is to a dolphin. You do not need to ask. You *know*."

Twilight had come to an end. Night came one star at a time; then whole constellations stepped forward. I turned my face to the soft evening breeze and was freed from melancholy.

El Gordito! I was beginning my own life!

I scampered faster than an iguana up the mainsail mast, to catch the rise of the moon. My arms and legs wrapped themselves around the warmth of the massive black timber, the neck of the swan. I closed my eyes and allowed myself to be rocked.

chapter

Birdie

I didn't plan to sleep on the trip at all.

First there was the drive to PDX—Portland International Airport. Mom drove a rented car since naturally we didn't want the Volvo away from home a whole year.

The ride there was the hardest part, two hours of winding roads after getting up at four-thirty in the morning. I was barely out of dreamland! Luckily I had my Discman and a fabulous Courtney Starz CD to keep me going. Plus a backpack full of computer games, a new sea-adventure paperback, stick-on glitter nails, pens and markers, and of course my journal. If I got hungry there were cheese crackers, M&M's, gum, Life Savers.

It took forever to get through security inside PDX, especially since we were leaving the country.

I sacrificed the window seat so I could sit between my parents and always have a fresh game partner when one wore out.

Halfway to Florida, we were served breakfast burritos, just like at home, plus bananas, milk, juice, bagels, cream cheese, jam, and yogurt.

I spent the second half of the flight sitting very still with my eyes closed, trying not to throw up.

MIA—Miami International Airport—was totally cool, a cross between another country and another planet. Mom had a tiny cup of Cuban coffee, ordered in Spanish. *Español.* Dad had a yummy *pastelito.* I'd recovered from overeating—actually I was totally starved again—so Mom took me across the terminal to a regular Taco Bell.

"Be careful," Dad called to us.

"We will!" we said together, and laughed.

The *chalupas* tasted way better than at the Riverton Taco Bell!

We got an eyeful, waiting for our Island Air flight. Everyone was tan or naturally brown, and the clothes were like from Hollywood—bright colors, slinky stuff; guys showing hairy chests, girls showing cleavage.

And then something 100% unexpected! Reporters rushed by us, hollering and pointing down the walkway. TV cameras were set up in a brightly lit area, and a pretty blond girl smiled, spoke into a microphone, waved to the crowd. She flashed her hair a lot, the way Kirin did.

She wore low-cut jeans and a short top. Her abs were tan, muscular, and fabulous. But it wasn't until a pack of kids rushed by us yelling, "Courtney! Courtney!" that we recognized her! *Courtney Starz,* model, singer, dancer, video star, right there in front of us! Someone said she was on tour, that she was going to London from here.

"Wow," Mom said.

"Wow," Dad said.

I didn't say anything, I was so starstruck!

Then we were pushed back, made to walk on, and that was that. The glamour exhausted me. After we boarded our plane, I conked out before we'd left the runway.

Next thing I knew, Mom was nudging me. I'd taken the window seat this time, and my heart leaped as I saw how we were rushing low over the water. It sparkled with shades of navy blue, turquoise, and a heartbreaking in-between color that you could only call Caribbean blue. A misty green island lay dead ahead.

"St. Maarten," Mom said, stretching. "Last stop before St. Petts."

SXM was a small airport, and our airplane a small plane. Instead of unloading into the terminal, we had to climb down portable stairs onto a cracked, grass-sprigged concrete ramp. I stood there in the open hatch, taking in the scene: slow voices, slow-waving palm trees, the slow movements of the Caribbean ground crew, taking their time unloading our baggage.

I shrugged into my backpack and breathed air that was warm, light-heavy, coconut-silky. The air here was like food! I drifted down the steps, paying no attention at all to the muttering crowd behind me.

I felt deliciously full . . . and at the same time, I craved something I had no name for. . . .

chapter

10

MORGAN

I cruised the populated waters off El Gordito, trying to find enough space to anchor. The sleepy little town had been discovered by tourists.

Hurricanes are only one of the troubles that come to Caribbean nations. There are poverty and dissent between races and villages, and issues of outsiders taking over. The same as it is in much of the world, except the sun is perhaps brighter here, the sand softer, and the coral reefs more colorful. The rich come to amuse themselves; the poverty is hardly noticed. I have watched tourists offer a girl less for her handmade hammock than for their flavored coffee drinks back home, and still persist in the sport of bargaining.

I anchored as far away from the holiday boats as I could, which wasn't far enough. The gaudiest of them, an American sailboat, was serving cocktails. The guests laughed in remarkably loud voices. The hull was fanned by its visitors' inflatable dinghies: silver slugs feeding off their fiberglass host.

"Come on over, sweetheart," called a large-bellied man

dressed in white pants and yachting cap. He swung his arm as if he could herd me across the small expanse of water between us.

I continued furling sail, checking the set of my anchor, looking anywhere but at the party.

He tried again.

"Hey, Miss Sweden! Have a drink with us!" Guessing wrong on the origin of *Svanhild,* or perhaps not knowing there was a difference between Sweden and Norway.

"Come, on, darlin'. One cocktail?" He cranked his voice even louder. "A Sveed-ish meatball?"

The other guests had begun to look over. I refused to look back.

"Well then, *how 'bout a hearing aid?*"

I was the source of laughter now, something I've never borne well.

I dropped my dinghy into the water, leaped into it, and took the first pull on the wooden oars. It felt good. I put my body fully into motion.

"Look at her go! No wonder she doesn't like you, Hal—it's a friggin' guy. A hotshot racer like at Harvard—"

I closed my ears to the rest. But how would I ever find a way out of loneliness, if I couldn't bear to listen to others? If I saw only flaws in my own kind?

How, Oona?

They are not your kind.

They are, Oona, they're *people.*

Watch for your kind.

You mean instead of listen?

Keep watch.

I sighed. Keeping watch was what I did day and night at sea. I was hoping for something more specific.

What I felt most like doing was walking. I'd guarded my parents so long, stayed so close to the boat and the bars, I felt great pleasure at going off on my own.

I pulled up to the pilings, tied the dinghy, and climbed to the dock. There had been many changes in El Gordito since the tourists had found it. Shiny new bars lined the marina and a Western Comfort hotel cast its shadow the length of the beach. Trinket shops were stacked with postcards, and T-shirts read, WE ♡ YANQUIS!

I quickly bypassed these novelties, rushed by the little repair shops and permanently broken boats at the outskirts of the harbor. The busy main street bustled with taxis, vegetable stands, grocery stores, vendors of beads, cloth, parrots, avocados, fish.

My legs were suddenly slicing like long-bladed scissors. I moved fast and without effort, hearing nothing of the crowd around me. It was as if I didn't exist inside the same space as the others.

My breathing was deep and regular. I was unaware of the odors that were surely there: greasy fried breads, sweating workers, the perfumes of roving tourists, unkept toilets. I strode on, heading across the boulevard, uphill through alleyways that finally became dusty pathways.

In fewer minutes than it takes to eat a mango, I was in a new village, in a new world altogether.

My steps slowed, my heart slowed, and I reentered the world. I watched a peasant child push two thin goats ahead of him. We stared at each other, exchanged shy smiles.

I climbed the small *gordito* hill and sat at its very top. On one side, I looked down at the deserted village, and on the other, at an adobe hut with a smoking cooking pit in front. Beyond it were a creek, two trees, a tiny green garden.

Farther: dry brown pastures, dry brown mountains.

A girl, not yet a teenager, walked toward her hut. She was barefoot, the dress she wore so oversized it was surely her mother's. She spoke to the only other creature around: a single white hen.

Her voice was soft and fond. *"Blanca, Blanca, que linda, Blanca . . ."*

She tossed her pet a handful of corn.

Invisible as a god, I watched the two kingdoms.

The village streets held nothing but a tethered burro and a few balding dogs. It was the very sort of place where Oona and I, after a storm, would have distributed beans and rice and tubes of antibacterial cream.

Back on the other side, the girl ducked through the low doorway of her hut. In a few minutes she returned with a round of dough in her apron. She knelt to form circles of uncooked corn tortillas that were soft and fragrant as baby flesh. My sense of smell had become keen again, or perhaps it was my imagination that had, but I was sure I could smell their musty goodness.

The girl was still a child, yet she was having to be the mother to a family who were somewhere—working on the docks or selling vegetables or hammocks in town. She faced the hillside but did not notice me. She was as dark and pretty as one of the tiny chocolate dolls they sold at the *mercado.*

She bent over the flame, her dress bunched around her ankles as she swayed from side to side, passing flats of dough over the flame, building a tall stack of tortillas.

I imagined her stuffing them with the little mounds of the filling she'd prepared: onions, beans, chilies, tomatillos, cilantro, goat cheese. Ready for her silent, rough-mannered brothers when they came home from wherever they were.

My mouth watered at watching her do what she did so well: making a lot of food from so little.

I swallowed and turned my gaze to the other side of the hill. The village was no longer deserted.

Three hungry-faced boys, each one a different mineral color—copper, iron, fool's gold—each one looking full of trouble, jostled down the street, bickering with each other.

The girl's brothers? I didn't think so.

Copper-boy had sly, brilliant eyes that seemed to miss nothing; if I were discovered on the hill, he would be the one. I saw he was the leader even though Iron-boy was strongest, arms long and muscled despite an unfed childhood. Fool's Gold was most handsome of the three. Over and over again, he picked up stones and threw them at dogs that easily avoided them: His mind was simple and mean.

I could see everything from here.

I watched them descend into an arroyo and follow the narrow sand canyon around the hill. They never glanced up at me.

Then they were there, right in the girl's yard. I was relieved to see she'd gone inside.

Fool's Gold kicked over her tortillas, then, thinking it over, bent to retrieve one from the dirt and stuff it in his mouth.

My eyes flashed sideways to Copper-boy, just as he set fire to the tail of the white hen!

I was on my feet in an instant, surprised at the depth of my outrage.

Its bokking shrieks brought the girl flying from her shack. Her fine-boned body was little more than a flexible pole inside the flapping dress. Her face was knit in alarm: Losing an egg-laying hen would be tragic for a family that had so little.

Copper-boy grinned, showing his ruined brown teeth, and motioned for the other two to grab the girl from behind. She had managed to catch her hen and smother its smoldering backside when Iron-boy jerked her off her feet.

I was already moving down the hill; I saw his thick features unfold with surprise at the lightness of the girl.

"*¿Vale la pena?*" he said.

Is she worth the trouble?

Fool's Gold stood aside, staring at the bareness of the girl's flailing legs. He was grabbing at himself in an animal way, both hands busy. He didn't even see me before I knocked him face to the ground.

I jumped over him, on my way to Iron-boy.

Iron-boy couldn't take it in, that I approached him so boldly. Was I going to *fight* him? He glanced twice at my chest, trying to decide if he was wrong: *This is a girl, isn't it? Then what's she think she's doing?* And then I saw a third thing, the thing that made me smile: *If it's only a girl, then why am I afraid?*

I don't like hitting, although I am very good at it.

I said, "*Váyanse, dejenla en paz.*"

Go on now, let the girl be.

He shook his head, but he'd also loosened his grip. The girl wept, too frightened to struggle.

I said, "It's all right, *chica;* I will kill them if necessary."

I'm very fast. When Iron-boy hesitated to obey me, I kicked his legs out from under him, lifting the girl from his grip as he fell.

He scrambled to his feet. With great sincerity, he cried out ugly names: *¡Cabrón! ¡Chucha! ¡Marimacho!*

Copper-boy had already fled for the shelter of the arroyo. He bawled instructions over his shoulder, "Stab her, cowards, do it!"

Iron-boy screeched back, "I have no *knife,* what are you thinking? If I had a knife this *yanqui* witch would be dead!"

I did not like being called a *yanqui.* I was a sailor, a *Caribbean* sailor, if distinctions were to be made.

My displeasure must have shown. Iron-boy raised his hand, guarding his head, and backed his way to the arroyo.

Fool's Gold was on his feet again, standing with mouth loose, arms slack at his side. I had only to slap him once. He cried out and was gone. All three were suddenly gone.

But Copper-boy would send them back for me, I knew that. And there would be a knife this time.

I held the girl upright and wiped her tears. She was slack as worn line.

"*Pobrecita,*" I murmured. "Poor little thing. Have you no mother to guard you?"

"No, *señorita,* nobody." Her eyes were immense, so black I could hardly see the pupils, the whites a silvery blue. "Just brothers mean as those boys—those boys are their *amigos*—and my aunt and uncle, but they live clear to Puerta Rosa."

On the coast.

"I'll take you to them. Hurry."

She had nothing to bring but a shabby, once-colorful shawl, in which she bundled her hen. We grabbed what remained of the unspoiled tortillas, handfuls of chopped onion, herbs, a small lump of fresh cheese, and wrapped them in a rag.

I said, "*¿Como se llama?*"

"Lita," she said shyly.

I grabbed her hand and we clambered over the crumbly surface of the hill like the runaways we were.

From the crest, I saw the boys below, excitedly speaking with two large-chested men. Others were gathering.

"*¿Gringo?*" one said in loud disbelief.

"*¡Uno yanqui bandolero!*" cried Copper-boy, unable to admit in front of the others that I was a girl.

He gestured to the hillside, and Lita and I flattened ourselves to the ground.

Bok, said the hen.

Lita whispered, "No, Blanca, hush . . . *cálmate,*" which somehow worked.

The men picked up shovels and stones and marched in a tight group into the arroyo, ready to slay the *yanqui* bandit.

An old woman remained behind, watching as the men disappeared. We rose to our feet, careened down the hillside with Blanca.

"Shhh!" Lita said to the old woman, put a silencing finger to her lips.

The old woman made encouraging little shooing motions as we raced for the pathway that led back to El Gordito and the docks.

I tucked Blanca under my arm. Lita held her skirts high, ran alongside me like a startled coatimundi. We reached town breathing heavily, entered the boulevard, slowed to mix with the crowd. The crush, the smells, now welcoming. We found a bench on the plaza and opened our flattened packet of food. Lita skillfully rolled the ingredients into delicious tacos, and we wolfed them down.

I bought iced limeades for us and Lita drank hers in one long noisy swallow.

"Moor-gan? Are we all right? *¿En todos?*"

"Yes, Lita, completely all right."

Her trusting smile, her expression warm and sweet as marzipan, made me want to rescue all the mistreated girls of the world.

o o o

Lita was a joy to have aboard the *Svanhild*. Blanca was less happy, confined by the crude cage we had rigged for her.

I'd rushed to get us away from the docks. Trouble with the

law is a very grave matter for a sailor. I purchased just a few groceries, topped off the water tanks with fresh water—suitable for bathing only—and we departed. I needed no new fuel; I rarely used the engine.

My visit to El Gordito was so quick, the harbor authorities had no chance to motor out and check my boat papers. Luckily! I belatedly realized everything was different now that I was alone. I was a traveler of undocumented age and nationality, and the boat registration was not in my name. Both things would have to be fixed before the next major port.

o o o

Lita was delighted by everything: rowing the dinghy, the tiny galley and the making of tea, the tilt of the deck when we were in motion—even sitting on a bucket to urinate made her laugh. Too soon we were back down the river and anchored outside the few buildings that made up Puerta Rosa.

Lita ran ahead of me. She knew the way to her aunt and uncle's blouse factory, with its small living quarters behind.

Inside the dark room, the uncle sewed fabric together with a sewing machine. Three women, the aunt included, hunched over his blouses, layering them with fantastically embroidered flowers and vines.

The chubby aunt leaped up and cried, "Lita, Lita, how can this be that you are here? Did your brothers finally let you come to us?"

Lita grinned, loving the excessive hugs that jerked her this way and that.

The uncle was less enthusiastic until Lita explained to him that she had a way with a thread and needle. And an egg-laying hen of her own!

"And I cook, *Tío*, real nice food. Tell them, Moor-gan."

"Real nice," I said.

I handed Blanca to Lita while the aunt and uncle stared at me top to bottom. The uncle finally offered his hand. Neither asked a question.

"*Adiós.*"

"*Adiós.*"

Lita had already disappeared into the back of the tiny factory, probably on the prowl for her aunt's famous *bizcochitos,* which she'd dreamed about on the trip up the river.

At the dock, a man in an official-looking cap, peasant trousers, and bare feet stood surveying my anchored sailboat as it swayed back and forth, the only boat at port.

Unsmiling, he stuck out his hand. "*Pasaporte, señorita.*"

"*Uno momento, capitán.*"

I signaled that I'd retrieve my papers with my dinghy, be right back.

Engines do have their purpose. Once on deck, I quietly retrieved the anchor, pushed the ignition button, and was gone before the *oficial* could close his mouth.

Of course he didn't come after me. He probably didn't even have a boat. His official cap was most likely something he'd found washed up on shore. He trudged away from the dock as if it always happened this way, and why hadn't he learned to collect money first thing!

Was that what made me laugh? Or recalling that look on Iron-boy's face when I came for him?

Or was it because I was finally living my life?

O O O

I traveled northward. Each day my thoughts returned to fixing my official paperwork. I recalled a man we'd sought to help us last year, when Mother was detained for fighting the coast guard. A shyster, Father had called him, known to fix problems outside the law. Not a pirate—we would never deal with a pirate or his savage practices—but merely a shyster. Paperwork was his specialty. . . .

I felt the wind and close-hauled the sails, adjusting my destination for the tiny private island where he resided. Calista, between St. Maarten and St. Petts.

Puerto Rico, and major provisioning, would once again have to wait.

At the St. Maarten airport, only the suitcases and two of our three trunks fit into the luggage compartment of the taxi. The third sat up front like a silent relative. The taxi was rusted and dented on the outside, and the lid of its trunk tied with string.

But the inside was decorated like a palace! The seats were upholstered in leopard-patterned velveteen. Red tassels hung from the corners of the ceiling and a huge crystal dangled on the rearview mirror and shot sparkles of light into our eyes. On the back of the front seat were pinned plastic roses and a complimentary partial pack of cigarettes.

The driver talked nonstop in English we mostly couldn't understand. It didn't matter. We nodded, squinting out into the brilliant light, watching people in every color. Shorts, sundresses, turbans, robes. Chickens ran along the sides of the road and goats and donkeys didn't seem to belong to anyone. I scooted closer to Mom, leaned my head on her shoulder.

She smoothed my hair; I inhaled the grassy scent she always wore; it gave me more a sense of being home than any town could do. Then we were at the dock, the spectacular sea spread out before us.

We unloaded at a handwritten sign that said CHINGO'S FINE 3-TIME-A-DAY FERRY TO SANTE PETTS. The final four-hour boat trip, and we'd be at our new rented bungalow for an entire year.

We kept speaking that thought out loud, like we were inside a dream, pinching each other with words.

It was almost noon, a day after we'd left Riverton. Only not really, because of time changes.

The taxi driver told us the ferry would be there any minute. We plunked down on our trunks and waited. A rambling marketplace was in full swing just across the road. Tables, racks, and blankets were crowded under a tangly banyan tree that shaded an entire block. On this side of the street was a little store, a shack actually, where they sold weird kinds of soda pop like Ginseng-Up! and Lemon Smacker. Deep-fried pieces of banana, other things, were handed out the window.

T'ings be han dot d'wind-o, in Caribbean-talk.

Fishing boats, tugboats, yachts, sailboats, passed us by. In the slip next to us was an eye-catching powerboat. *Cheater* was printed along its long elegant side, and every detail of the boat— would you call it a yacht?—looked well tended and expensive.

We had a long time to notice the *Cheater*'s details. Nearly an hour and still no ferry. We were restless, and without our packed-up hats, we were starting to sunburn. We looked up at the sound of every motorboat, but none pulled into the empty space.

A well-built young man in a wide-brimmed hat called hello from the fancy boat next to us.

Actually what he said was "G'dye, mates!"

An Australian! My favorite kind of person! He jumped gracefully down next to our sprawl of luggage.

"Getting toasted down here, are we?"

"Yep," I said. "Like shrimps on the barbie!"

He grinned, his smile as dazzling as a movie star's.

I saw that under his hat his hair gleamed pale blond.

Mom was smiling at him in a way that told me she thought he was pretty cute too. She said, "I'm Clara Sidwell . . . my husband, Henry, our daughter, Birdie."

"You own this boat?" Dad said. Then, not waiting for an answer, "Impressive. But why's it called *Cheater*? What's that mean exactly?"

I could tell he'd been dwelling on this.

"Well, I s'pose it means cheats the wind, doesn't it? With her big engines and such. Moves right out when you ask her."

"Mmm," Mom and I said, goofy smiles on our faces.

He was wearing a bandana around his neck, which I would have thought completely corny two minutes before. But his outfit was as perfect as his boat: khaki pants, a gauzy—but manly!—white shirt that looked brand-new. And his very tan, very appealing face beneath the down-under hat.

"Sorry to disappoint," he said, "but if old Chingo hasn't come by now, he won't till seven tonight."

He gazed out of *killer* eyes, large, dreamy, and the same dark brown as an innocent seal pup's. A long scar ran across his cheek, but even that seemed handsome. He was someone who'd known adventure. Maybe even *danger*.

He said, "That '3-Time-A-Day' sign is a bit of a brag. Fellow doesn't have a brass razoo, but he'd rather go for a kip than make a coin." He made a snoring noise, so we knew a kip was a nap. "It's how they are down here—but come aboard, have an Orange Crush."

We could easily keep an eye on our things. We trooped up his ramp to the deck. We did as he did and slipped off our sandals. The polished wood was too perfect to scuff! Then we went below, which surprised us as much as the inside of the old taxi.

The main room was practically spacious! Golden woods curved around to form cool shadowy nooks, and there were red leather benches in a U around a marble table. Tiny lights glowed down the hallway. There was a red leather sofa and a small kitchen that was perfectly spotless. The bedrooms—cabins—were closed out of sight.

One corner of the boat was lined with technical-looking equipment, digital cameras, and every kind of computer gadget. A built-in desk was being used for an art project, maybe a collage. Scissors, glue, squares of paper were neatly arranged.

"Oh my," Mom said.

"Wow!" I said. "I could live here, no problem!"

"Could you?" he said, looking so closely at me it was like he thought I meant it.

I looked just as closely back at him. How could a scar be so attractive?

He suddenly pulled off his hat, his hair longer and even blonder than it had seemed, and put his hand out to Mom.

"Nicholas Rigby," he said. "I lease this slip year-round; come back and visit anytime. Except you probably won't, not once you dig in at St. Petts; it's wicked nice there."

Wicked nice. I'd be putting that in my journal.

Dad was frowning. I thought he was just lost in his own thoughts until he said, "Cheats the wind, eh? I'd think someone could have come up with a name not quite so . . . objectionable."

"Too right, mate!" Nicholas said. "I threw a wobbly when I bought her, wanted to change it straight off. D'you suppose it means a little something different, one place to another?"

"Cheater?" Dad said. "I don't think so . . . that's a bad thing anywhere."

Mom and I were staring at Dad. We'd never heard him go on like this; it was just *rude.*

"Honey?" Mom said to him. "Want to take a walk? Go sightseeing, have dinner, we've got a ton of time—"

"Our stuff would be stolen in two minutes, Clara, and we can't lug it around."

"I should have offered!" Nicholas said. "Leave it on board, go have a gander, take an early tea—be back by seven, though; that's Chingo's last run."

"How kind of you!" Mom said.

Dad gripped his laptop to his chest and shook his head. "No thank you."

"Dad? Please let's! I need some things from the market. Mom, can I have one of those orange-and-pink vests? Did you see them? At the first stall?"

"It's up to you, honey. You have your own money. But don't spend it all first thing—"

"Stick around, mate." Nicholas gave Dad's shoulder a thump. "Let the girls blow off. We'll have a coldie, play some poker, get you sorted out."

"Henry?" Mom was smiling. She was no doubt wondering whether her husband would choose shopping with the girls or beer and poker with the boys. I don't think he'd ever done either in his life.

"I guess I could check out the produce," he tried. "The indigenous legumes . . ."

"Good idea, honey. Beans . . ." Mom was already headed up the stairs—the companionway—and I was right behind her.

"Thanks, Nicholas!" I said, doing my best at glancing back adorably while tossing my red curls.

"She'll be right, bugalugs!"

Whatever that meant. At least it got him smiling that killer smile.

"Only thing—one little beastie—got to top off the petrol today." He cocked his head down the docks. "Over there, you can just see the tanks."

We looked. "Mmm." Not a block away.

"If I'm not here, I'm there."

Nicholas hefted our luggage on board himself, stacked it inside his cabin. He had awesome muscles, like he worked out constantly. Maybe driving a luxury yacht around *is* a constant workout.

"G'dye!"

"Bye, Nicholas!"

Dad took his laptop with him and headed straight for the vegetable stands.

"Bye, Daddy. Meet you back here in an hour?"

"Henry, are you sure you want to drag your laptop along? You don't want to leave it with Nicholas?" Mom asked.

"No, I'm not leaving it with Saint Nicholas. At least I'll have my computer when he sails off with everything we own. Laughing all the way!"

"Oh, Henry, he's rich, and he *lives* here; he doesn't want our things. . . . Birdie, did you notice how dark his eyes were? Do you think he's part Aboriginal?"

"*Unbelievable* eyes, Mom, and his eyebrows are so pale they almost disappear, except in the sun they're *golden*."

"Oh, for heaven's sake!" Dad said. "Goodbye, Birdwinkle; goodbye, Clara. If you haven't already run off with Mr. Universe, I'll see you here in an hour."

Boy, he was in a mood! He turned and struck out on his bean quest, not even bothering to call, "Be careful."

Mom shrugged. "He does look like a bodybuilder, doesn't he?"

"Who? Dad?"

We laughed all the way to the tree-shaded stall where a small brown family sat weaving amazing orange-and-pink vests.

○ ○ ○

I only bought one thing: the vest. It was perfect. I doubted I'd ever take off: my wearable memento of the first day in the Caribbean. I slipped it on, wanting nothing more than to stroll, and to look, and to take pictures of everything I saw.

Except my camera was back in my suitcase, wrapped in the top layer of clothes. It would be easy to get, even Mom thought so. I ran toward the dock to retrieve it.

She called, "I'm going to meet Dad, honey; it's time. Come straight back to the banyan tree and we'll go for supper."

I was starved! I planned to order chicken and rice and beans and tacos and a mango shake, if such a thing existed. And then eat a handful of the tiny chocolate dolls we'd gotten at the market.

Instead of just jumping onto the *Cheater,* I called out, "Permission to come aboard?" Like they did in my seagoing novels.

Nicholas was on deck, shirt off, closing up a can of brass polish. He'd pulled his pale hair back into a short ponytail, and it gleamed in the sun.

"Bugalugs! Look at you in sunset colors!"

I blushed, avoiding looking him in the eye. Instead I found myself staring at his chest! It was overwhelming, being so close to someone so cute and so big and so . . . *masculine*! I smelled his sweat, which last year would have made me gag but now seemed weirdly interesting.

He must have been at least twenty-five. That made him ten years too old for me even if I had been fifteen, the age at which I planned to fall in love. Sigh. He'd just have to exist in my journal.

He was squinting at my face. "You know you're going to be a

great beauty in a few years, don't you? Maybe not tall, but your face, your coloring, are lovely. . . ."

I thought I would faint.

"My camera," I squeaked, and scrambled below.

He called down, "I'm headed over to the gas tanks, don't lose your balance."

"Aye aye, captain," I said.

Aye aye? Who was I, Pippi Longstocking?

I was as dorky as Nicholas was cool. I noticed he'd said gas instead of petrol, doing his best to communicate with an American girl.

The engine, two engines, roared to a start. Above me, through the portholes, I saw masts go slowly by as we pulled away from the dock. I pulled my camera out from between a sweatshirt and a layer of underpants and was bounding back up the companionway when I heard Nicholas calling over the engines.

"Bugalugs? Look, the folks are waiting at the dock. Want to take their picture?"

Great idea! The First Day, would be the caption of the photo. I'd use it on the cover of my Perfect Year scrapbook.

They smiled and waved. I clicked.

We were almost to the fueling dock when something else clicked: Nicholas was doing an amazing American accent—was it just for me? Or was he an actor? He was sure cute enough.

"Good accent, Nicholas! Are you—"

"Wave back, Bugalugs—Mom and Dad look worried."

"Yeah, they're worriers." I waved, pointed toward the fuel tanks.

Only we'd passed them. In fact we were headed toward the open sea.

In the few seconds it took to glance away, my parents had become distant figures. Only their frantically waving arms set them apart from the scenery.

Nicholas slammed the throttles forward. The nose of the boat lifted as we leaped away from the last of anything familiar.

"Say goodbye, Bugs. You won't be seeing Mommy and Daddy anymore."

He turned to me, hand moving to his face. In one motion, he ripped the scar from his cheek and held it up.

The strip of rubber dangled from his fingers like a centipede. My eyes stretched open as the waggly thing filled my vision. Was this all some horrible kind of trick?

I frantically searched the horizon for my parents.

Gone!

Nicholas bugged his eyes at me, savagely mimicking my expression.

If I'd screamed, it would have been lost inside the roar of the engines. But I didn't scream.

chapter

12

MORGAN

The shyster's name was Nicholas.

Yes, *Tricky Nicky* is how he was known to those who lived as we did: those unshackled by petty land laws—unless suddenly entrapped by them.

Nicholas was all the name I had, but I supposed it was enough. It wasn't as though his services would be listed in a telephone directory.

I remembered Calista well. The privately owned island was lovely, though hardly larger than a sand spit. Mother speculated on how it came to be that its owner, old Peter Vunderweer, a recluse and a millionaire, would let such a person as Nicholas reside there. But the discussion went no further. Mother was facing the coast guard and time in prison. For that brief period, she and Father lived in a barracks, under guard. Both of them sober, frightened at how their lives had come to such a dismal place.

I was sent out to find a man who was only a rumor, a last hope. That was a year and a half ago. I was sixteen. The incident had occurred on St. Croix, bad waters for legal issues: United States Territory.

Calista was only a few days' sail from St. Croix. The travel was the easy part of it.

The miracle was that I'd found him at all, and that—for half the money we had in our accounts—he'd produced a document with a White House seal. He told me he guaranteed his work, and we saw that he did. A few days later he managed to intercept the coast guard's questioning of that document.

Mother was freed.

Things changed rapidly after her release. My parents were barely recognizable to me without their magnificent cloak of self-confidence. Even their great physical stature seemed to shrink. They began to age.

The next drunkenness was the deepest. . . . They were never to surface. . . .

I sighed. Below, at the navigation station, I connected to the Internet by satellite. I smiled in relief: The day before, they had made a small withdrawal from the account I had set up for them!

My hands shook with emotion. They were functioning! Using money in their frugal custom, adjusting to new circumstances. By checking in this way, I would be able to keep a distant eye on them. I felt proud of their small accomplishment, withdrawing money, and saw how little I'd come to expect of them.

I wished it were as easy to solve my document problem.

Oona?

Oona, is this the right way? To fix our papers?

You have already decided.

Have I decided right, though?

If you have decided, you have decided what's right, for your-self.

Would Oona be surprised to know how like Mother she was? It seemed like I was getting fewer and fewer direct answers from her. Surely she knew how much I counted on her for instruction? Without my sister, I would be lost. I feared her silence over all things.

o o o

I sleep by napping, at times when wind and weather allow. Even then, to close my eyes for a few minutes means a chance of collision, in even the emptiest of seas. Or the chance of cyclonic waterspouts tossing us aside. Or, what happened with Oona, a storm's afterwave, raising its water-fist for a death blow—

It was bound to happen.

Yes, Oona. The unexpected.

So unless we were becalmed, or were trapped in weather too heavy to attempt control, I rarely slept in my berth. I was a perpetual outdoor camper, atop my own little wooden campground.

It was early summer, a time when storms were rarely life-threatening. Hurricane season begins in August, ends before the day of my birthday mark, the shortest day of the year.

Today, we were becalmed, a rare occurrence in a trade-wind sea.

I sat at the edge of the boat, undressed except for a lengthy rope belt. The end of the coil was tied to a stanchion. My legs dangled free, toes wiggling as I marveled at the sea's change. The surface was utterly flat and clear. It was as though the *Svanhild* had come to land on a giant green pond. Fish and turtles rose to the surface in a way I had never seen.

I could look *into* the sea, and I did for some time.

Oona? came the unbidden question.

Did I think she was *in* there? Living in there, all this time? Of course I did not, my mind was a rational one; I did not believe in ghosts. Then . . . what?

I touched my rope belt for reassurance and jumped into the water. I did not care to dwell on these questions.

I've read, in the many moisture-wrinkled novels stored on board, how people jump from their boats into the sea to have a refreshing swim. Real sailors do not jump into the sea for any reason. To be separated from your ship means death. In thirty seconds of moving sea, you can be gone from your ship forever. I had only done such a rash thing once before, with Oona. I was doing it now only after great consideration.

The skies told me no change was at hand.

I wore a rope that would allow me to easily climb back aboard.

The sea would likely stay the same—although the sea never promises.

The shock of cool water made me laugh. I dived deeply, felt

the sweet pleasure of the sea sliding against me. I held my breath one minute, another, forcing my body downward. Suddenly the depths flashed with silver—five, six flashes—and I was in the company of dolphins! The sisters and brothers Oona had most sought! They smiled their permanent smiles, checked their speed so I could join them. At 268 counts, my limit for not breathing, I was forced to surface.

One followed me. A young male. I don't know how I could be so sure of these things, but I was.

The boy-dolphin butted me. I laughed, pushed back, and he was gone and back again before I could move aside. He gently grazed his teeth along one arm. Nibbled at my hair. Playing!

I passed my hand along his back, over his sensitive fin. He made a thin cry, slid under one arm, rough silk, then back between my knees. I rose on his back and for seconds we were free of the water. We flew! We crashed back onto the surface, the crash harmless to the dolphin, but stunning me.

Suddenly I was being dragged deeply, violently below the sea! My rope had painfully encircled boy-dolphin's tail, panicking him. He dived straight into the bottomless sea to escape it.

The rope ran to its end, nearly jerking me in half as it caught. I felt the sway of the boat above us. I thrashed, a mere snarl in the rope—caught, like Oona, inside the sea. Below me, boy-dolphin plunged again and again, like a hooked swordfish.

Each lunge pulled the rope tighter around my middle. I grabbed at the rope above me, trying to pull us up before I passed out. But of course I could not bring up the weight of both of us. I kicked at the rope below. Tight as wire. Boy-dolphin did not feel my jerks; he felt nothing.

I saw how easy it was to die, if you were Morgan Bera, and you lived at sea.

Oona, help me!

Oona!

Call to him!

It made no sense, *calling;* we were underwater! But I could struggle no longer. I gave a great water-scream and a block of bubbles burst from my lungs.

The rope instantly went slack, and he was there, pushing his nose against my belly. We rose swift as rockets to the surface.

I caught my breath in great bursts of laughter. I was alive! I was exhilarated! I had feelings too large for names—all given to me by my boy-dolphin.

I loosened the rope at my waist, then tugged it free from his tail.

"My brother . . . ," I murmured, and tenderly stroked the abraded skin around his tail.

I pressed my forehead to his, pulled back to look into his black eyes. I saw myself there, my own eyes solemn and huge, broadly distorted in the silvery reflection.

Suddenly I was exhausted. Taking his dear face between my hands, I tenderly kissed the edge of his mouth. When I pushed away, reached to haul myself aboard the *Svanhild,* a terrible cry of loss broke from him. My heart ached more than my battered body at having to leave him behind.

I slept on deck until an evening breeze rattled the rigging. The trade winds had returned!

My bare skin was burned and I had a terrible nausea and salt-thirst. A storm-black bruise spread from my belly to my breasts, and it hurt to draw a deep breath. I rose carefully, gulped fresh water. Not bothering to rinse the salt from my skin, I dressed. The boat wallowed chaotically until I raised its sails, turned it to the wind.

Our journey resumed. There is no real stopping at sea.

Boy-dolphin followed for two days. I could no longer join him. And then he could no longer follow. Dolphins must travel together; it is their nature.

I was alone again. I wept, an unfamiliar sound, longing for company, for love, for my own kind.

O O O

I stayed far off the shores of St. Croix and kept my eyes peeled for signs of coast guard ships. The *Svanhild* was on record now. A second brush with the coast guard, after my mother's troubles, would go badly. I decided I was close enough to Calista to blindly try for Nicholas on my sideband radio. I intended to repeat my calls intermittently for the next few days, and to begin making inquiries about how to reach him. His was a kingdom not open to surprise visits.

"Nicholas, Nicholas of Calista, the *Svanhild* calling."

Instantly a familiar voice crackled back. "*Hell*-o there, *Svanhild*. Would that be my favorite teen buccaneer? Your folks in some kind of trouble again?"

I almost fainted at the unlikeliness of reaching him! As if he were a genie riding the airways, just waiting for his name to be invoked.

His young handsome face bloomed vividly in my memory. The fine blondness of his hair, so like my father's; the beard, trimmed down to a heavy shadow. He'd kept sunglasses on the whole time, but I suspected even his eyes were nice to look at.

I recalled how the scar at the base of his throat evoked images of a suffering past. I was sixteen then; sympathetic.

His presence filled the boat. I'd forgotten how I'd struggled not to be overwhelmed by him, not to become suddenly demure and pleasing. Even his voice was compelling. I was very uncomfortable with these powerful feelings.

"Uh, yes—yes, it would be me. Over."

"Sail on over; tell Nicky all about it. We'll have iced cappuccinos, get it straightened out."

"I . . . all right." He made it all sound simple. Like it was virtually done! "Estimated time of arrival, two and one half days. Um. Over and out."

"Gotcha."

You *don't* have me, is what I wanted to say back. But I wasn't quite sure about that.

The wind picked up and the sails thumped like beating hearts. We would arrive early if the winds stayed this strong.

I smiled and turned on the radio. An hour of Jamaican music would go well with my feelings.

chapter 13

Birdie

I should have jumped, I should have jumped, I should have *jumped*!

It's like the words were written inside my eyelids, ruining the one place I could hide.

Mostly, those first days, I was as sick as I'd ever been, throwing up and thinking the same thought over and over again:

If only I'd jumped!

The water Nicholas gave me was poisoned. I knew that, but it was so hot in my berth I had to drink it anyway. I slept a lot, woke up with a headache, threw up, thought about where I was, became terrified, drank water, went back to sleep. My cubbyhole was like a grave, a dark underground slot creaking and thumping with the boat's motion: endless, sickening—*endless! Sickening!*—rolling back and forth.

If only I'd jumped!

There'd been time, that first moment when we were still close to the harbor. Once I *knew*. I might have gotten hurt, but I also might have gotten free! Now I never would! Never! I had no idea where we were. We'd been moving around the ocean for days, and we weren't even in the same boat we started in! Even if all America were looking for me, the entire coast guard, they wouldn't find me now.

My eyes were raw from crying, and my insides ached from hours and days of pure terror. I kept telling myself, *you can't drown a Duck*. I wanted to be an example for my team! But breathing deeply and thinking positive thoughts were not enough. I wanted my mom. I knew I was being a baby, but more than once I'd awakened hearing my own tear-muffled words, "Mommy, I really, really need you. . . ."

o o o

Nicholas knew what he was doing. His kidnapping technique was perfect. We'd talked about it in my classrooms, how it works when you're kidnapped or mugged or hijacked. It begins with a shock so severe you can't get over it.

"You won't be seeing Mommy and Daddy anymore. . . ."

How did he know that for someone like me, those words were equal to an act of violence? Had he figured out our family so quickly? When had he decided to do what he did? And *why*?

I didn't even wonder about those things when it happened. His words, the furious power of the engines, my parents almost instantly disappearing from sight . . . that rubber scar *thing* . . . I was shocked senseless.

I had no thoughts of saving myself, or of stopping him. I had no *thoughts*. I'd been reduced to pure unbearable feeling.

"Go on below, Bugs," he'd said calmly. Not a trace of mockery left in his voice, nothing but a thin white sliver left on his cheek. "There's a nice cold drink for you in the fridge, tropical punch. Drink it all, take a nap."

The push he gave me down the companionway was almost playful.

I staggered down the steps, did everything he told me. It was like I was already dead.

○ ○ ○

I can't say how long it was before we first changed boats. Not very long. Nicholas made no secrets of anything in front of me. That fact would have frightened me if I'd thought about it. A man thumped on board, and then Nicholas was handing over the boat to him. It seemed like it was a done deal, something arranged before me.

There was laughter between them.

"Woo-hoo, blondie! Don't you look cute!" a man joked with him.

Money was counted out.

The first poisoning was the strongest. I was paralyzed for the boat exchange and hardly cared. Nicholas had wrapped me in a sleeping bag, hoisted me back up the stairs, and laid me next to my family's suitcases. A gigantic woolly-legged spider strolled across my chest and I was no more disturbed than if it had been a maple leaf. A trunk—two trunks?—were tossed overboard, other things. I heard them crash into the water and waited to be tossed in after them. I was too far gone for it to matter.

Then Nicholas packed up a neat stack of his own things: his fancy cameras, the art supplies, his nice wardrobe. A red racing boat was tied to the side of the white boat. Brought by the new owner? It was an open boat, sporty, very long and pointed, like something in an Austin Powers movie.

Nicholas exchanged goodbyes with the man on board and then carried me down the rope ladder. His arms were warm, rounded with muscle. He was very, very strong. My head lolled against his chest, his heartbeat immense in my ear. An extrastrong heart? Made of steel . . . of kryptonite? Then I was lying alongside the rest of the cargo, my mind looping unreliably between alien sights and sounds.

The next thing that happened is strangely vivid to me: At the last moment, he reached to peel the name *Cheater* from the side of the white boat. It came off with a long ripping sound, and I was reminded again of the horrible rubbery scar. Under *Cheater* was written *Denise,* or *Danielle,* some regular woman's name.

Nicholas carefully lofted the heavy plastic sticker in one hand and then, as if it were a giant Frisbee, flung it into the sea. For a moment, it floated on the surface of the water, glimmered in the starlight like a cosmic warning. My eyes rolled toward him. He winked at me, and then the plastic sank. He gunned the motors of the race boat, and we were off again. It turned night, but we kept on. Our speed caused us to crash furiously up and down, smacking the water's surface.

Several times he flashed a powerful light into the darkness. Finally he whistled and said under his breath, "*Hell*-o, beautiful. You'll do."

He cut the engines, called out. I felt the rolling lift of water, the watery silence, and could only imagine we were far from any shore.

An old man called back. His first words were German or Dutch, and then English.

We gently bumped into his boat.

Nicholas hollered up, "My little daughter and I, we're adrift. . . ."

An old woman cried, "Ach . . . poor child."

Nicholas climbed aboard.

I wanted to warn them, but I couldn't make a sound.

Then—were there shouts? A scuffle? Maybe . . . I can't be sure.

Nicholas dropped back into the race boat, unrolled several lengths of heavy black tape, and carefully smoothed them over the old name. Anklebutter—Enginebiter—something . . . it was dark, my eyes unable to focus.

"Right as rain," he murmured, and gave the boat's hull a thump.

Then he leaned into my face and grinned. Even in the dim light, I saw that something had changed. His eyes, once brown as the bottom of a grave, were now the drowning blue of the sea.

Contact lenses? I was too far gone to put it all together, to ask the questions that would come later.

"Ho-kay, Bugs," he said, nodding at the new boat. "This is a major score. I knew you were lucky, little ladybug. Upsy-daisy."

Up onto the deck, down into the cabin. He pushed me into a small berth. *Did the old couple take the red boat? Or did Nicholas just cut it loose?* I wondered, and then my thoughts vaporized into sleep.

○ ○ ○

Over time the poison became weaker, although I couldn't remember eating anything or going to the bathroom. Of course I must have, but nothing is clear, those first days.

I got over the seasickness, but not my anxieties. There was no sameness, day to day. I was kept in different beds, or on the floor, or tucked onto corner benches. Nothing was ever still: We ceaselessly rocked or lurched or heeled to one side. The portholes were covered over, day just a version of night. And most disconcerting, through my personal haze, Nicholas himself was changing. One day his shining blond hair was shorter, then came dramatic dark roots, and then it was very short and all-over dark. Wavy. His eyes had already gone from brown to blue. His scar-track tanned into oblivion. And the thing that changed him most of all—his eyebrows! When they were pale, his face had an innocent, even angelic sort of charm. Now they'd grown in heavy and black—or been dyed, I didn't know—but they were fierce and powerful over his navy-blue eyes. He was altogether changed, but the changes had left him more handsome than ever. His beauty was an unfaltering thing.

The changes didn't seem gradual. I knew they must have been, but my brain was working in a pulsing, on-off way. Time hopped instead of flowed. I threw up on my pink-and-orange vest, blinked, and was miraculously dressed in clean clothes. A blond Nicholas was brushing my teeth, a brunet Nicholas was asking me to rinse the toothpaste out. Rubber scars chased scowling black eyebrows across my deranged thoughts.

I yearned to drink something unpoisoned. To gulp pure water from the tap. Or a cold fresh lemonade! But the same bottle was always waiting when I opened my eyes, the first thing I'd reach for. And then the craziness would begin all over again.

Finally Nicholas began to appear as the same Nicholas, time after time. His face the only familiar sight. His voice the only familiar sound. Repeating over and over what he called *facts of life;* insisting I mumble each phrase back to him:

> *With the death of the past, the future is born.*
> *A princess obeys her prince, always.*
> *The only true family is the family that's chosen.*

And then he'd launch into his *simple rules of safety:*

> *Never go in the water without a buddy.*
> *Never drink water stored on the boat.*
> *Always use mosquito spray before sundown.*

Sometimes he'd tell stories to prove his points. He said that recently a beautiful movie star had visited an island not two miles from where we'd sailed. She'd been too lazy to use bug spray.

"Of course that evening a mosquito got her, and she came

down with malaria. No more sunsets for her, Bugs. So sad how people can die by not following the rules."

In the silence that followed, I thought about that.

And then there was the one about the adorable beagle puppy who drank shower water on someone's boat and two weeks later grew a brain tumor so large it actually came out his velvety little ears.

Even drugged, I doubted the stories. Still, the words wiggled like earwigs inside my head. I knew that unless I was instructed otherwise, I would became more vigilant at sundown, and that when I showered, I would keep my lips sealed against the water.

○ ○ ○

Then the toxic bottles of water became no more than simple sleeping medicine. I was always groggy, but aware now when Nicholas dressed me or helped me go to the bathroom or fed me. My thoughts began to broaden, and to seem more like my own. . . .

I was mortified at what he must have seen when he was doing things I no longer even let my own mother do. But he was always so matter-of-fact, other worries soon crowded those thoughts from my head.

More than anything, I was stuck on the regret of not jumping from the boat when I was first kidnapped. It circled my head like a witch on a broomstick.

It all came down to one thing: I had let myself get captured.

I sighed, took the smallest sip of water, and suddenly felt an overwhelming urge to pee. I believed I was strong enough to try sitting up. If I could do that, I could surely figure out how to get out of this hateful little room. My tongue stuck to the roof of my mouth. I was forced to reach for the water bottle again.

Nicholas was singing up on deck. He did that a lot, sang to himself. He was maybe the most cheerful person I've ever been around. And he was definitely a non-Australian! I'd heard him talk to others, and he never said a single thing like "G'dye, mate" or "Have a coldie."

Using a fake accent was just part of tricking us. Although why he'd tricked us, why he'd kidnapped me at all, wasn't clear. Yet.

I was trying to reconstruct everything that had happened, trying to find some hint of where I might be. But it was hopeless! Tears leaked from my eyes. I just couldn't make sense of it. I'd been too sick and too drugged, time was all twisted inside my head, along with strange memories that might actually have been dreams.

I didn't have a clue about anything. If I ever got to a computer, I'd have to e-mail Dad and say,

```
I'm on a boat, not the same boat as
before, a big black sailboat, SOMEWHERE
IN THE OCEAN. I am hopelessly lost.
Love,
Birdie
P.S. Nicholas, my kidnapper, is American.
He doesn't have that scar anymore. He has
```

```
big black eyebrows and blue eyes, and he
doesn't look anything the same.
P.P.S. If the coast guard has given up,
you might as well go ahead and adopt a
similar child.
```

I saw that my attitude sucked.

Buck up! I told myself. There were things I could do! Like pay attention to everything. Keep track of clues, and of days that passed. So far, I'd been too out of it to know how long it had been since it happened.

I decided to count that day as my first day of *knowing*.

Rolling heavily over on my side, I tried to make a mark in the teak wall with my thumbnail. My arm shook with the effort, dropped back to the bed. I had no strength at all. I promised myself that as soon as I could move around, I'd find a way to keep track of the days.

I took a deep breath and reminded myself how special I was.

"I must stay brave for Mom and Dad." My voice was slurred. "I must be an example for the Ducks . . . and for Riverton."

My legs and arms trembled as I lifted them one at a time— lowered, lifted—trying to make myself stronger.

If I lived long enough to write stories again, I could use all this for material for my book! Heinous, preposterous, and gruesome things had finally happened to me—

The tears were back. I saw what a little girl I'd been, an immature little girl—shallow, the complete opposite of deep— to have ever wished for such things to happen.

The engines suddenly slowed. Nicholas brought them down to an idle . . . and then switched them off. We'd landed somewhere!

The silence buzzed in my head. I struggled to sit up.

I heard light footsteps, some quick efficient chore he was doing above.

For some reason, I thought we might be in Australia. That maybe Nicholas's fake accent was all about wanting to be an Australian. All I'd need was a peek to know. Sydney, Australia, was famous for that giant white building on its shoreline.

I breathed deeply, waited for a moment of dizziness to pass.

The door of my berth burst open.

"Bugs! You're up! Just in time for lunch—come on, brush out the cobwebs! How's a cheeseburger sound? A big frosty mango shake?"

His face filled my horizon. It was like I was watching his radiant smile on a movie screen. Rhett Butler swooping down on Scarlett O'Hara. I blinked: It must be the drugs.

"You'll need a shower! Untangle those curls!" He stretched out his hand to me. It was like he was saving me from what happened, my best friend to the rescue. I suddenly couldn't make the connection, how it was Nicholas who had done all this to me.

"Come on, Bugs." Voice gentle as the sway of the boat.

I was suddenly starving, and desperate for a shower, and needing the bathroom.

I took his hand.

◦ ◦ ◦

And that's how I began to learn the rules. I was the puppy, the pocket pal, who would be lavished with toys and affection and yummy tidbits—as long as I remained housebroken and obedient.

But the price for rebellion, or even ignorance, was harsher than anything you'd do to a puppy! I learned that quickly, and after that, terror was never far away.

After a shower in our new black yacht, a bigger, plainer boat than the other, I dried off with towels embroidered MUETI and PAPI. I felt the dizziness return for a moment: the old man and woman, *"Ach . . . poor child!"*

What had become of them? Or were they just in my imagination?

"Come on now, Bugs," Nicholas called, like he could read my thoughts through the door.

I sat at a smooth wooden table inside the boat. The companionway door was closed, leaving it dim inside. I sipped a fruit smoothie as he gently combed out my tangled hair. I was shaky but feeling better than I had since it all began.

For the first time, I'd completely dressed myself. It happened naturally, both of us knowing without discussing it that I was now strong enough. He'd picked out clothes, had them waiting for me in a neat pile after my shower. He busied himself in the galley while I dressed in as much privacy as you get on a boat. I managed to do it, but my arms and legs were loose as rubber bands.

I stared down at my outfit as he combed my hair. New clothes from my trunk, purchased for St. Petts.

Is that where my parents were now? Or were they still in St. Maarten—or in a boat out looking for me—

"Ouch!"

Nicholas hit a snarl, deliberately pulled at it.

"You have that 'Where's Mumsy?' look on your face, Bugs." He'd lapsed into his Australian accent again.

"Where *is* my mother, I need—"

The comb was embedded in my hair. When he jerked it, my whole head snapped back. He held it there.

His face loomed upside down over mine.

"Those thoughts won't do, will they?" He jerked again.

Bad puppy!

"Ow! No—" I was crying again. "No, they won't do!"

He gently raised my head up, blew little puffs on the sore spot.

"There . . . all better?"

His smile was . . . mocking? Apologetic?

I was so confused. And I felt nauseated again, and sleepy.

"Did you . . . did you . . . put sleeping medicine in the smoothie?"

"Sleep's good, Bugs." His voice was hypnotic, kindly. "Sleep's very good. Here, upsy-daisy, who's ready for a little nap?"

I was. I was very ready for the end of lesson one.

○ ○ ○

I woke in the black boat, of course; it promised to be permanent. But I was in a different berth now, and I could tell by the gentle motion that we were still anchored. This room was spacious, more like a small bedroom. There was a porthole, but, as usual, it had been papered over. A little wall fan rotated a cooling breeze back and forth across my face, and on a shelf waited an unopened (unpoisoned!) can of Pepsi, sitting in a bowl of melting ice. (Good puppy!) I reached for it, popped it open, and gulped. I was clearheaded enough to get up right away and try the door. Locked! (Bad puppy!)

I knocked on it and listened as Nicholas's footsteps tapped down the companionway.

"Bugs!" he cried.

Why did he have to call me *Bugs*? The only creatures I wasn't fond of.

"Look what I have for you here!"

My cherished orange-and-pink vest, clean and folded!

I reached for it. "Actually, my name's Birdie—"

He jerked the vest behind him.

"I don't think so, Bugs. I don't think that's your name at all."

He slammed and locked the door and didn't come back until the next morning. I'd wet the bed and was crying, miserable and humiliated, when he opened the door.

"Bugs?"

I nodded.

"A shower?"

I nodded.

His smile was warm as sunshine.

"I'm cooking us a *fantastic* breakfast, and then we're going ashore and get you acquainted with a very special place. Okay?"

I nodded.

"Okay?" he said again.

I tried smiling.

He handed me my vest.

○ ○ ○

I was being Nudelized. Or Nicholized. It was all the same thing: bullied, brainwashed.

I thought about Kirin, how it must have been for her, how it was for her again. *Knowing,* but unable to do anything but go along. All you could do was pretend and try to keep your real self hidden. Is that how Kirin had done it? I'd given her so little credit for what she'd been through!

Poor Kirin!

Poor me!

Was no one going to help us?

chapter

14

MORGAN

The first day a helicopter came over, I thought nothing of it. I'd seen many of them before. The only frightening incident had been a year earlier off the coast of Colombia. Military men sat in the open hatch, dangling their booted feet. The helicopter lowered until I could see their leering faces. One raised his gun to me and sighted me in.

I'd scrambled below, where my parents' snores filled the cabin, and grabbed a mechanical bow. It was what my family kept for protection. There was always the chance of pirates boarding. Every boat needed defense, but it was not good, if you were caught, to have a gun on board.

The thumping blades of the helicopter mimicked my pounding heart. I leaped on deck and raised the loaded bow to them. The water churned around the boat, pelting my face with salt water.

The man put down his gun, and they all laughed, pointing at me, making mock arrow-shooting gestures. The helicopter roared off, vanishing in seconds. It was just a moment of fun for the bored *soldados,* probably out seeking drug runners.

Today's helicopter was also military, the U.S. Coast Guard. My hands turned slippery on the wheel. If I was boarded without my new papers, I would be arrested. I would be returned to my parents in Panama, the *Svanhild* possibly impounded. I'd heard stories of sailors' losing their boats in just such a way.

What if they had heard my broadcast to Nicholas? Perhaps they were stalking him, perhaps anyone who called him was suspect! I'd identified myself: announced *Svanhild* into the airways—how very stupid of me!

Nothing could be worse, for me, than to be trapped and put into a small jail cell! I could not bear to imagine it—

I took a deep breath. The helicopter, a small but official-looking craft, swung close overhead. I saw its pilot survey my deck, return for a second, closer look. And then it was gone.

Would it send a coast guard boat for me?

I reviewed my radio conversation. Nothing had been revealed. And how likely was it that officials sat monitoring the affairs of a small-time shyster such as Tricky Nicky?

I had overreacted. In another day I would have my papers and again be a fearless citizen of the world.

Later that day an identical helicopter, different crew, passed over me. The pilot was solemn-faced. His copilot searched my deck with his binoculars . . . for signs of what?

I was unnerved.

chapter

15

Birdie

Nicholas stood up on the deck, pulling the paper from the outside of the portholes, squatting to Windex them sparkling clean. Inside, I stood on tiptoe and peered past him. If we were off the shore of Australia, there was no sign of Sydney on the horizon.

Our island wasn't close to anything but water.

When I was brought up on the black yacht's deck, I looked at it and said, "Is this an Australian island?"

It just popped out, leaving me hoping I wouldn't be punished for asking.

He smiled broadly and ruffled my hair. "Close, Bugs. Very close: one of the Cook Islands. It's called Calista, too little for any map." He studied my face as he spoke the next words. "We're a long way from Kansas, Dorothy—halfway around the world."

I swallowed but kept my face neutral. I only had a vague idea of where the Cook Islands were. Not that it mattered! We were a million miles from anyplace American helicopters would look!

Would my disappearance get special attention because of

Dad being such a favorite in Washington, D.C.? Would his amazing bean knowledge be enough for the president himself to get involved? I wondered—and then caught myself.

Nicholas was frowning at me. No doubt I was wearing that missing-my-mumsy look again. I touched the sore spot on my head and tried to distract him.

"I was just wondering, Nicholas. Are you an artist? Is this your retreat? Where we'll be living?"

"Yes, little bug, aren't you brilliant at figuring these things out! I *am* an artist"—he bowed—"and this *is* our retreat. Yours and mine—you'll be my inspiration and my lucky ladybug. Royal Princess of Calista. I'll get richer every day, and you'll get more beautiful."

He did a little dance step and swung me around him. Naturally he was a great dancer. I was relieved our conversation was going so well.

"Prince and Princess of Calista!" he said.

I laughed. I couldn't help it. . . .

○ ○ ○

Nicholas was right about one thing: It was very special here. It was the way I imagined St. Petts would be, only there were no towns on Calista. You could walk around it in half an hour. Every trail and building and decorative bench was done just right. In fact the whole island was as clean and deliberate as if invented by Walt Disney himself.

On the quiet bay side was a single wooden dock, a few maintenance and storage sheds. A graceful tile-roofed home sat on a knoll above the beach. It had been stuccoed the exact same color as the sand. A big porch wrapped around three sides, and a tidily painted, new-looking sign had been tacked over the doorway: CHEATER'S PALACE. A joke? A family name? I didn't ask.

Most of the island was jungle. It gently rose from a sandy bay and ended with a cliff on the opposite shore. It was much wilder over on the cliff side, windier, the surf banging against the rocks. In the center of the jungle was a shanty where Nicholas's "worker" lived.

I was shown all this on our exploratory hike. Nicholas had insisted I wear long pants to keep from getting my legs scratched. And I had my backpack on. Since Nicholas had given it back, I'd hardly taken it off. It had all my familiar things inside: my journal, Discman, books.

Nicholas loved the idea that I was a writer. "Aren't we the dynamic duo, Princess! I just knew you were special."

I guess I was a little off balance from wearing the pack, because I tripped on a stone ledge, pitched forward.

Nicholas grabbed my arm. "Whoa! Watch it, Bugalugs—"

I peered into a deep stone pit—an empty well—almost invisible under the heavy cover of ferns and brush.

"It goes down forever," he said. "This is a wild place, Bugs. That's why we have a stay-out-of-the-jungle rule here on Calista. Only when I bring you—got that?"

I nodded. Danger everywhere. In Riverton, only if you crossed against the main light could you put yourself in danger.

"My helper lives out here. See his little house?"

It was just a shanty made of various materials that included old boards and even cardboard. It was built on the stone foundation of an old ruin and was the only thing I'd seen that wasn't perfect.

Vines thick as trees wound themselves up the ruin's crumbling stone walls. And there was some kind of ancient machine—awesomely huge wheels and cogs—that had long ago begun falling apart. Had this been a sugarcane plantation? Were the Cook Islands once cane farms, like in the Caribbean? I was so ignorant of anything outside the United States.

Nearby, neatly parked in a metal garage, were tractors, a small backhoe, a truck, a couple of old Jeeps, a small fishing boat, and a ton of other things I guess it took to run an island.

Nicholas ducked inside his helper's shanty and brought out a thin scowling man, maybe fifty years old. He wore loose trousers and no shirt and had the very black skin and round face of some of the people I'd seen in St. Maarten. One hand gripped a massive machete as though he was never without it.

I supposed the Cook Islands were also populated with Africans that had been enslaved? I wished I'd paid more attention to world history—not to mention geography! I knew Tahiti had brown-skinned people. I'd seen lush Polynesian paintings in the Portland museums. I'm afraid they stuck with me more than history and geography.

"Bugs, meet Bajo." Nicholas nodded at him. "He has his own kind of brilliance with engines, motors, whatever. Keeps things running, looks after Calista when I'm gone—"

Nicholas broke off, leaped at the porch, shattered a loose board with his savage kick.

"Crappy carpenter, though."

Bajo suddenly spun his machete overhead, leaped forward, and brutally chopped the head off a giant fern.

My hand flew protectively to my own head. Both men laughed. Whatever was going on here, I didn't understand it!

I spoke in a timid voice. "That's a big sword, Mr. Bajo."

He scowled.

Nicholas made some tight signs with his hands and Bajo trotted off in the direction we'd come from.

"Stone-deaf," Nicholas said. "Born like that. He gets by fine, but he's got a vicious appetite. I brought him a cat for company once and he cooked her. Keep away from him."

My mouth was still open as he led me back into the jungle. All I could see was Fat Silly being chased around a barbecue pit.

"Did he really eat her, Nicholas?"

He grinned. "You'll never know, will you, Princess?"

I wouldn't know a lot of things; I was beginning to see that.

o o o

Nicholas kept the black yacht anchored out in the cove—Cheater's Bay—instead of at the handier little dock where his motorboat was kept.

One afternoon he motored me out to it for a "little down-time." I hadn't asked for downtime, so I supposed he meant it was for him. He hadn't shaved for a couple of days and the effect was so dramatic, it spooked me. I didn't want to think about what the beard meant. Changes meant danger. So when

145

Nicholas gave me an entire issue of an American teen magazine, color-printed off an Internet site, told me to go below, read it, have a Pepsi, I did so quietly.

When I heard his motorboat head out to sea instead of toward the dock, I didn't even look out. I figured he was going to the closest point on Australia, or to another Cook Island, to do whatever he did besides steal kids.

I sat in my berth and flipped through the bulky stack of computer paper. The banner said July, but I knew magazines always came out before their dates. I'd been marking down the days in my journal—most of the time—but something had kept me from adding them up. I dragged my journal out of my backpack, turned to the secret page.

We'd left Riverton the end of May. If I had to guess how much unknown time passed when I was drugged, I'd say between one and two weeks. Ten days is what I'd call it. I counted the marks out loud: thirteen marks, plus ten before that . . . plus a few for the days I forgot to mark down. That took me to the third week of June.

Almost a month.

I dropped back onto my pillow. A very long time.

My kidnapping would no doubt have been on TV, but at this point it was old news. If I were to judge by rescue efforts, I'd been forgotten entirely. Of course my parents would never forget, but how long could they keep an official search going? People got bored with long cases, stories that didn't have quick, dramatic endings. Or at least exciting clues that popped up every once in a while. I was pretty sure Nicholas didn't leave much in the way of clues.

TV people were shallow! People who *watched* TV were shallow! I pushed the pages off my stomach, watched them scatter across the floor. Magazines were no good without glossy pictures anyway.

I had more important things to do with my time.

Like what?

I braided a strand of hair. Raised my legs over my head and kept them that way, bare feet planted on the wall behind me. Observed that I desperately needed a pedicure. Peered out between my knees for a while, studying the not-very-interesting teak ceiling.

I was so bored I wanted to scream.

Eventually my mind came up with some entertaining ideas. I pretended I was on a grand cruise. A hundred years ago. A ship like the *Titanic*. I was a brand-new bride, in my teak-ceilinged berth.

Sentences formed in my mind. I lowered my legs to the bed, allowed the scene to take over:

The burnished gleam of rare wood curved above our ample berth and cast a golden light on our skins. My husband, lying beside me on cream-colored satin sheets, turned his handsome head to look at me. I saw myself reflected in his misty sea-green eyes: I was an exquisite beauty in a silk nightdress the same cream color as our sheets. I knew my beloved husband would now make me his wife, and that afterward we would nap comfortably together. . . .

I paused, regretting that I didn't know many details of sex beyond the napping. Instead, I'd add more description to the nightgown! It was suddenly as vivid to me—the ribbons, the antique lace—as if I were wearing it. I reached for my journal, began writing my story out.

When I had written *The End*, I turned over on my side and slept.

○ ○ ○

I woke with a calm mind and began evaluating my situation.

So far I'd discovered that Nicholas's real last name was *Vunderweer*. That hadn't taken much cleverness. The words *Peter Vunderweer* appeared everywhere from the brass door knocker to the title under the gigantic portrait of an old man in the living room. I supposed Peter was Nicholas's grandfather.

I guess even when Nicholas first introduced himself, he knew he'd be kidnapping me. Or else why would he have used the false name of Nicholas *Rigby*? And why had he been in disguise? This week's beard made me wonder if he always left the island in disguise.

And why had he taken me anyway? I still didn't know!

I turned to a fresh page in my journal and began a list of possibilities.

1. Because he will get money for me.

2. Because he is weird.

3. Because he is lonely and needs company.

4. Because I will be beautiful in ten years and he is willing to wait.

Number four seemed far-fetched, even to me. Number three was a possibility, because anyone can be lonely. Except usually you don't steal someone for company.

The first two were most likely, because, number one, Nicholas made it clear he loved money. And, number two—the scariest reason—he *was* weird.

I knew it was even more than weirdness. I mean, Mrs. Kimball was weird, but she wasn't dangerous. Not really.

I didn't want to write down or even think about how weird a guy would have to be to steal a kid from her parents. How Nicholas was as on-and-off as an alarm clock.

I knew all this, but I guess I thought if I kept acting like things were sort of okay, they sort of would be.

I wanted money to be the number one reason he took me. He would put a price on me; my parents would buy me back. Maybe the government would help. It was just taking some time to arrange.

I could deal with that.

o o o

Nicholas came back late that night. He was clean shaven, eyes bright with success from his trip to who-knows-where. My own eyes were bleary from heat and getting woken up.

"Pick up the pages, straighten your berth, little piggy. Let's get back home."

I nodded sleepily, did what he asked.

On the ride back to the dock, I had to sit on cartons of

groceries and cans of fuel. Nicholas had ripped open the packaging of a new cordless electric shaver, and had obviously used it on the way back from wherever. There was a new KitchenAid mixer with a box of angel food cake mix in its bowl, a ribbon around it all. The tag said, "For My Bugalugs."

I was in no mood for his bribery. I peered inside a shopping bag brimming with books and financial magazines and periodicals. Maybe there was a newspaper—

"Looking for newspapers, Bugs?"

I frowned.

"I get my news on the Internet. If you want the news, just ask me."

"I do want it."

"No you don't. You just want to know if you're in it. You're not. Not anymore." I could feel myself crumbling. I was too sleepy for this. "Anyway, why would we want to be bummed out by the news, when we could be baking." He pointed his chin at the KitchenAid. "Ta-da!"

Thank goodness we were at the dock. I had no smiles that night, not even the fake ones that seemed to work so well around there.

o o o

Basically, the guest room of the main house was where I lived now. I say basically, because Nicholas liked to switch things around. Soon as I had the routine figured out, he changed it.

He loved saying "A rule is a rule," but he changed the rules around as easily as he did everything else.

Yes, I could walk on the beach by myself.

("Of course, Bugs. You live here, you're family. Do anything you want!")

But no, I couldn't go into the jungle.

("Uh-uh. Even I can barely see that stone well. Can't have my girl falling in, cracking her little head in two.")

Only one rule was absolute: I was never to go into his art room.

He said his art was a very private thing.

I suspected it had more to do with the fact that the phone and the radios and his computers were all kept locked in there, but I didn't say that.

Instead I asked him, in what I hoped was an irresistibly appealing voice, "Can my journal fall under that rule too? It's my private place for words."

"Sure," he said without thought. "Doesn't it say 'Private Journal'? Main thing is for you to keep writing. You and I have special destinies, Bugs."

I nodded and said thank you. But I knew we didn't have the same destiny in mind for me.

○ ○ ○

One of our variations in routine was to both sleep on the boat. When we did that, he brought over delicious foods and bottles of juice and a portable video player. We'd set up a movie on the foredeck, eat chips and dip and stuff. Then he'd make me sleep below in my hot berth—"Use the fan, pill bug"—but he'd spend the night on deck in a hammock, binoculars on his chest.

I never actually saw him sleep.

"I get a kick out of being under the stars like this, Bugs. Keeping watch from our own little hidey-hole."

Keeping watch for what? Did he have news of my rescuers?

The times he left me alone on the boat were way different. He dismantled the navigation station so there was no risk of my contacting anyone when I was alone. He always turned off the fuel to the stove; disconnected the water.

"I don't want you tempted to drink that water, Bugs." He waggled his forefingers on either side of his head like they were beagle ears and raised his eyebrows, silently asking, *Do you remember the tumor story?*

Yes, I remember that stupid story. But I didn't say that out loud.

He usually left me good old Pepsi to drink. Sometimes a six-pack of a stale-tasting canned water called Aquarium. Something local, I guessed. I imagined goldfish lurking in the bottom of the cans and didn't drink it unless I was out of everything else.

A kind of walkie-talkie was rigged between the house and the boat. If I was on the boat by myself, I wasn't to leave it without permission. I wasn't even supposed to come up on deck without contacting him by walkie-talkie. Mostly he made the rules seem like a game.

One day that I'll never forget, I thought I heard him calling and went up on deck without asking.

It was just a seagull, crying out as it circled.

Nicholas must have been watching, because he immediately motored out in the little boat. I squinted as he drew near. Was I imagining a thin white line on his cheek? Had he been using the fake scar again? Had someone come to Calista in the night? Or had he gone somewhere while I slept? I supposed that was why he had me out here. . . .

I worked at not frowning. "Hi, Nicholas. I came up—I thought I heard you calling."

"Did you, Princess?" He climbed up on deck. "You thought you heard your prince calling for you? But you didn't think to try the walkie-talkie?"

He smiled again, tossed me a mango.

I caught it, seeing too late one side was totally dripping rotten.

"Yuck! This is—"

Then I noticed his expression! My chest tightened when I saw the rage.

He grabbed my outstretched arm and yanked me to the edge of the deck.

"*Ow*, Nicholas, you're hurting me—"

"Stupid wench," he muttered through a clamped jaw.

He picked me up by my clothes and violently threw me overboard. I arced through the air, hit the water flat.

(Bad puppy! Very, very bad puppy!)

He leaned over and watched me, his face suddenly calm.

"A rule is a rule, Bugs."

I tried to gasp as I sank, but the wind was knocked out of me. I panicked, flailed in the water. I sank again, everything in slow motion. I looked up at the surface, watched the rotten mango float by, every detail of it gruesomely underlit by the innocent glow of water.

I kicked my way up again and wheezed, *"Help!"*

Nicholas dived overboard, plucked me out of the water, and gently lifted me into the motorboat.

"There we go, Bugs, easy, little one. What is this, you suddenly can't swim? You swim like an otter! Take a breath now . . . deep breath."

I couldn't. I was having an asthma attack!

He suddenly looked as panicked as I was! He nodded and motored us full throttle to shore, the boat's bow lifted high in the air.

"Don't move, be right back."

I sat propped against the side of the boat, gasping like a freshly caught fish.

He was back in an instant, fitting an inhaler into my mouth. "Okay now, you know what to do."

I did. It had been a long time, forever, since I'd needed it, but I released the medication and did my best to get some of into my lungs. With each shallow hitch of breath, I was able to take it in a little deeper. My lungs rattled, but I was breathing. My body began to relax.

I said, "Where did it—"

He shook his head.

I knew anyway, where it had come from. I could see my name on the prescription stuck on the inhaler. He'd been through Mom's suitcase before he threw it overboard! Good old Mom, of course she'd bring medication. Just in case!

Or was it good old Nicholas, for keeping it, for saving me from suffocation?

I was so mixed up! My eyes started to close. I'd forgotten how exhausting these attacks were.

From old habit, I tried to stick my inhaler inside a wet pocket. I'd have to keep it with me all the time now.

He shook his head. "Uh-uh, Bugs."

It was like he could read my mind.

He plucked the inhaler out of my hand. "I'm always close by. I'll always take care of you. Just a few little rules, so easy. Why do you make me scold you?"

Scold? I thought, and watched him pocket the inhaler.

Scolding used to mean a few words when I didn't pick up my room. Now it meant being thrown overboard! Maybe it wasn't a long fall, and maybe the water was warm, and maybe I was already used to swimming in it. But when you don't know it's coming, it's like . . . a flying pot of geraniums! A missile hurled with heinous anger. And it's *terrifying*.

I struggled to keep my face from crumpling.

"Poor Bugs." Nicholas combed my hair back with his fingers.

He made up a cot in his art room, which he usually kept

under lock and key. He kept a close eye on me all morning, propping me up for sips of juice. He worked steadily on one of his projects, hunched over it, careful not to let me see his work.

Once I woke from napping and found him gazing at me.

"I'm thinking of naming the boat after you, Bugs," he said. "What do you think of that? *Princess Bugs?* Kind of cute, isn't it?"

The room was tidy and perfect, like everything in his life. Each color of paper, each box of pens or unit of high-tech equipment had its own gleaming stainless steel drawer, cubby, or stand. Several computers were set up in the corner, all of them beige except one.

"Wow," I wheezed. "An orange Mac."

He grinned (good puppy!), pleased that I appreciated such things.

The odd thing was the Mac sat on a square pink case. I'd seen Le Cosmétique cases like this one at Nordstrom, expensive makeup cases that held a rainbow of glittery products. The fancy leather kind like this cost a fortune. It was what every girl wanted for graduation.

Was Nicholas one of those guys who wore dresses and makeup in secret? I didn't think so. I stared at the case, oddly disturbed by its presence. It certainly didn't belong to Peter Vunderweer—

I glanced at Nicholas, flinched when I saw him staring at me, staring at the case. His thick, perfect brows were knitted nearly together.

I closed my eyes, and my mind.

○ ○ ○

One day he brought out my snorkeling gear (good puppy!), and we kick-floated over near the underwater reef. I lost myself in that fantastic world. The colorful tropical fish and waving plantlike creatures were beyond anything I'd ever seen on TV.

"The Cook Islands are *amazing*, Nicholas!"

He laughed. "Yep. That's what they say."

We hardly lifted our heads out of the water all morning.

He had made me wear a T-shirt over my bathing suit so my back didn't get cooked. He was very careful with me in that way.

At the last minute, he brought up a crawfish-looking lobster. He knew I liked seafood and made a point of fixing it for me. He knew a lot of things from observing me so closely over the last month.

For lunch he made delicious lobster tacos. And instead of a green salad, we had the tropical fruit salad he'd invented for me and which we always prepared together.

Today he put on a reggae CD, loud, and we danced around the courtyard waving our arms and being silly.

Afterward, we flopped down on the beach. He was relaxed and feeling talkative.

"I tell you my deepest thoughts, Bugs," he'd said once. Sometimes those thoughts were a big surprise.

Like during a relaxed moment on the beach when I'd timidly asked him about the way he looked when I met him.

"So you think I looked different then?"

I hedged. "Well, my memory isn't perfect; it was so long ago—"

"So long ago, huh? Like how long do you think?"

"Umm, months?"

I didn't want to let him know I was keeping track. That it was probably July now. It was just the sort of thing he'd punish me for. Even asking these questions was risky. But he just smiled.

"Yeah, I looked different," he said. "My hair was sun-bleached. And I'd had a run-in with an iguana; it scratched the devil out of my cheek."

"Oh."

Only if you lived on the sun would black hair turn pale blond. And didn't he remember ripping off the fake scar in front of me? And what about having brown eyes then?

We stared at each other a minute, and then he laughed wildly, gave my toe a friendly pull. "Hey, when I go out, I like to dress for the occasion. Okay? Boys like to have fun too—"

The laughter stopped cold. He drew his magnificent brows together, looked deep into my eyes.

"The main thing you need to know is that this is my real self, Bugs. How you see me now"—he made a circle around his face—"what I'm sharing here with you"—he pointed to his forehead—"this is the real Nicholas. You know him better than anyone."

I thought this might actually be true.

Today was another of his sharing days. He loved the beach and the sun and was at his best when he was working on his tan.

He adjusted his face toward the sun, sighed contentedly. "This is what it's all about, kiddo. I just needed a princess for my kingdom." He rolled onto his side, spoke earnestly. "I'd like a whole collection of princesses to populate Calista, keep lonesome Nick amused. Someday I might even find a queen . . ."

His voice trailed dreamily off. I frowned. Why did everything he said leave me feeling wrenched in opposite directions? Why did he need more like me? Just me had been enough for my parents! And why wasn't *I* queen material? *Not that I wanted to be . . .* did I? It wasn't as though I *liked* being here . . . did I? No! I absolutely didn't!

And why did that Le Cosmétique makeup case suddenly appear inside my mind, flapping open like a pink leather mouth trying to tell me something? If there had been princesses here before me, they were surely back safely in their homes now?

Don't even go there, I said, being firm with myself. *Are you deliberately trying to scare yourself?*

○ ○ ○

We had a lot of those beach-lounging conversations. Nicholas's favorite part was asking me personal questions. He'd listen carefully, prompt me for every detail. But like with everything, he had rules.

I was never allowed to refer to the past. My name, where I was from, that I was missing anyone: All those things were punishable. I was supposed to be forgetting who I was.

But anything I felt in the present, my wishes and hopes,

anything about how I viewed him (well, the complimentary things)—he loved that.

"So what do you most wish to accomplish in life, Bugs?"

I assumed he meant besides getting out of here. "Well, writing my book, of course—"

"Your book." He smiled, approving. "Action, adventure?"

I nodded.

He said, "I'll be in it, I suppose?"

I knew my cues. This was suddenly not about my wishes, but his. "Mmm, yes, you will. The handsome hero—"

"Really?" He propped himself up on an elbow. "What will I do?"

I'd never seen him so pleased.

On the spot, I began to make up a story about him. Word by word, chapter by chapter.

When I said, "End of the first part," he asked a million questions about what would come next. This gave me clues for what my next chapters should include.

"That's all I have, Nicholas. My brain's empty. A story has to have time to build back up."

He accepted that.

It was the first time I'd had any power over him. I stretched out on my back and dug my toes in the sand. I was suddenly feeling very self-confident.

"What's it mean that everything's called *Cheater* here, Nicholas?"

He grinned, reached for more tanning oil.

"It's the key to success, Bugs. A trick here, a trick there, cheating puts you ahead of the game."

"Is that like a family motto? Was it your grandfather Vunderweer that named the bay Cheater? And you're keeping family tradition?"

He laughed until he rolled around in the sand. His muscular body and thick dark hair looked sugar-dipped. His intense blue eyes crinkled with fondness for me.

It disturbed me that a person's beauty could have such power over me. Kirin had fascinated me in the same way.

"Oh, Bugs, you're too much; you are going to be a great writer with that imagination! Seriously, though, it *was* Grandfather Vunderweer who named the bay; he was the greatest cheater of us all—how else could he have gotten all his money? Or an island like Calista?"

He jumped up, kicking sand and chanting like he was nine years old and back on a playground:

Grandfather Vunderweer,
Wearing dirty underwear,
Named his bay,
And went away—
Now I—I—I— (He thumped his chest like a gorilla.)
Am here to stay!

That evening, Nicholas asked me to write down what I had of his story so far, so he'd have it forever. It would take up dozens of pages in my journal, but I didn't mind too much because it was my best story ever.

I said, "But then I'll tear the pages out for you, okay?"

"Hey, your notebook's private, that's the rule. Don't worry."

He gave me a brotherly bop on the shoulder. "Everything's going to be all right."

Every little ting gonna be all right. It seemed like a million years ago that I'd been in the car with Mom, listening to Bob Marley sing those words. I didn't even know what worries were back then! I'd suffered over *rain*!

Nicholas stood in one smooth athletic motion, brushed sand off his arms. "How about grilled cheese for supper? Then we crank up the machine, make ginger ice cream?"

My favorites! "Thank you, Nicholas!"

I actually felt like hugging him—and then, like in a horror movie, I saw myself drowning. The taste in my mouth went from ginger to sea salt.

Why was it so hard to remember who Nicholas really was? He'd thrown me overboard! He'd brought back my asthma—an enemy I thought was dead. What was wrong with him?

What was wrong with *me*?

Why was I so susceptible to believing him?

I fought to keep my feelings from showing. He could read faces—minds—maybe even the future!

My nerves were shattering!

He sensed even that and changed the music to soft, mesmerizing sounds, as though we were in the company of distant angels. The wholesome, soothing aroma of lavender followed, although I couldn't tell where it was coming from.

The evening slowed. I was almost calm by the time we finished making ice cream. It was the best I'd ever had. That upset me all over again. I didn't want Nicholas's treats to outdo my parents' treats! In fact, I didn't even want Nicholas's treats—but I didn't want him mad at me either!

I remembered that phrase he used when he was pretending to be Australian: *wicked nice.* I thought it was cute at the time, but now it just seemed like who he was, a two-sided person, wicked/nice—

Just as I was thinking this, Nicholas asked me to pack up for a couple of days. He said I was going camping.

My heart sank when he loaded me into the motorboat and we headed for the yacht. I was in for a long hot boring stay inside it, is what he meant by camping.

He helped me up, lugged a black trash bag behind us.

"Sorry, Bugs, it could be a few days."

My eyes filled with tears.

"Look, though, Princess, *ta-da!*"

From out of the trash bag, he lifted the orange Mac. "Use it to finish *The Adventures of Naughty Nicholas.*"

He set it up over in the corner by the companionway.

The last thing I wanted to do was write an ending for his stupid story!

"Don't call this time, Bugs. The boat's charged up, Pepsi in the fridge. . . . I'll be back when I'm back." He tossed my inhaler in the air, caught it, and slid it into his pocket. "Practice not getting sick for a change. Asthma's psychological, you know."

He smiled, tapped his head, and stepped outside. I heard the lock click into place.

I glowered at the stupid orange Mac. Working at a monitor with the boat swinging around would no doubt make me puke!

Besides, I was sick of using my special brain for his story! It was my special journal! 100% mine! *Only!*

I was having a temper tantrum, a bad thing for asthma, but at the moment I didn't care. I pummeled the pillowy sofa with my fists, then kicked its velvet shins. It felt good, hitting things! I tried bashing a few other things around the boat, but all I got was stinging hands. Except for a small pile of towels, the boat was bash-proof.

I sat down, worn out, overheated. But for the first time since I'd been stolen, I was thinking clearly.

How dare Nicholas keep referring to himself as *naughty*? Like the things he did—stealing me—stealing boats, were *naughty*! Like he was a little boy playing pirate, instead of a full-on criminal.

Something was snapping in me. I could feel it. Things weren't all that complicated once I saw Nicholas for what he was: *a bad man.* Acting nice some of the time didn't do a thing to make up for the evil fact that he'd kidnapped me!

I decided to write down this brilliant revelation so I'd never forget it again.

Nicholas is bad, I wrote. *Nicholas can NEVER be trusted! Nicholas is tricky!* I scratched *tricky* out, wrote *crazy.*

Seeing it written down made me realize it was true.

Nicholas *was* crazy.

The truth was scary: I was the prisoner of a maniac and nobody was rescuing me. I'd have to be very clever to get out of this. Like Kirin, I'd have to live inside a fake personality. I was on to him, but I couldn't ever let him know. When his temper flared, he hurt me.

I added a note to my revelation: *mad = bad*.

Having been sighted by the coast guard helicopter turned things around in my head. Instead of my usual wariness at coming upon land and having contact with outsiders, I eagerly pulled into Calista's little bay. A refuge—

Except there was a coast guard helicopter landed on its shore, blades slowly idling! Two uniformed men bent earnestly over a sheet of paper, then looked up at Nicholas for a long moment. Like identical twins, they shook their heads back and forth, snapped up arms in salutes, and climbed back aboard. They swooped low over a black sailboat anchored in the inlet, and even lower over me, then saluted in a friendly way!

My heart would surely give out if I had any more surprises!

I searched the shore but found no other irregularities. It was difficult to remain vigilant in such a charming place. Old Peter Vunderweer had made a fine home for himself! It was much talked about in the Caribbean, that a man of such wealth had chosen the life of a hermit. I smiled, thinking we were of one mind in that way. Life here seemed to offer everything a human being could want.

Or did it?

Perhaps he was lonesome here.

Perhaps that's why he had so surprisingly allowed Nicholas to be his guest? To seemingly take over.

I would ask Peter, if I saw him this time. I would ask him, as one hermit to another, if he'd found himself lonesome . . . as I had felt.

The black sailboat was familiar. As I drew closer, I remembered its exotic radar gear. The *Engelberta,* the Bright Angel. I recalled the sweet-faced woman, her gray braids tied up like a silver crown.

Only, no . . . there was no name at all along the black side.

Boats were always named—or at least numbered. It was an international law. Most sailors took pleasure in making the choice. Perhaps it was just an identical yacht with identical equipment? Hmm. With its particular radar arrangement, not likely.

I dropped the sails and jumped down to the nav station.

"Nicholas, Nicholas, the *Sva*—" I caught myself. "I'm here," I said simply. "Over."

"I see you are, Buccaneer—and you brought some unwelcome company with you. Can't say I appreciate visits from the coast guard, Bucky. Well, tie up at the dock, come on up."

I blushed at his voice, and at the accusation.

"I didn't bring them—"

"Don't worry your pretty little head, they're searching for someone, a young girl—"

Nicholas heard my sharp intake of breath.

"You think they're after you?" His voice was bright at the possibility. I was determined he should not know my fears.

"No." I hoped my voice did not reveal the falsehood of this. I also hoped the coast guard was not listening to us. This was not a conversation that should be held on the radio.

"Actually, Bucky, you're right. They're not after you. Or me. This's about a kidnapped girl. They've got a police sketch of the guy who took her—someone with a serious scar on his face." He laughed softly. "My only scars are from broken hearts."

"Scars . . ." I was very relieved the coast guard wasn't looking for me, a mere girl without papers. It was a far graver crime they investigated.

"Anyway," Nicholas said. "They're gone, nothing here for them. Tie up now; I'll be glad for some company."

I nodded: I too was ready for company.

I glanced down at my shabby denim shorts and thin shirt. Should I put one of my father's old business coats over my clothes, carry his clipboard to shore with me? After all, I was here on business.

I imagined myself that way and a short sound broke from my throat. Even I could see that would look ridiculous.

But perhaps I might have a shower in Peter Vunderweer's house? I shook my head at the boldness of such a notion. . . .

O O O

"You're like me, Bucky," Nicholas said, tapping a pen on the gleaming metal surface of his desk. "Except of course you're gorgeous."

He grinned. He was of course the attractive one, but I understood that this was his manner of speaking. He looked very different than I remembered him.

When I mentioned my surprise, the absence of blondness, his clean-shaven face, he said people always said that about him, how he looked different from time to time. He said it was a family trait, turning blond in the summer. And that he was quite glad to be rid of his beard.

It was no wonder. His face required no hiding. Dark hair, stern black brows over winsome blue eyes: He was a perfect-looking man. And he was flirting with me. We had finished with the tense part, the discussion of fees, my handing over of the money. American money, the kind everyone liked best.

The amount he charged surprised me.

"It is far less than before," I said.

"We're friends now."

The words so simple, I was disarmed.

Afterward, surprisingly, he offered to sell me Calista! I took this to be a joke—surely the island was not his to sell! And then he proposed I buy the black yacht. When I shook my head no he tried again: He would make an even exchange, his black boat for my white one.

"I know that boat," I said. "It was called the *Engelberta*—"

"Nope-nope-nope." He shook his head as if I had no more brains than an eel. "It's brand new, never been named. There's lots of fish in the sea, Bucky, lots of big black boats."

This talk made both of us edgy. He tucked my money into his desk, and with the closing of the drawer, brought business to an end.

And now he was flirting.

He leaned back in his chair, stretched his powerful tanned arms over his head, went on, "You're just a little itty-bit naughty, too, aren't you, Bucky?"

I looked down. I was unused to this sort of talk. And there had been the wine he'd poured, cold and clear, even a few sips intoxicating. I made a small sound, a kind of laugh. Was I giddy?

"Naugh-ty Nicky and Bad Lit-tle Bucky," he said, the words slow and captivating.

Naughty Nicky certainly had a nicer ring than *Tricky Nicky*—as if he were a daring little boy.

It occurred to me that Nicholas saw me as a fellow outlaw. Was I as bad as he was, as naughty, because I had asked him to do something illegal? I supposed I was. . . .

We gazed into each other's eyes for a long moment.

"Hey!" He jumped up. "I'll get you fixed up right now, turn you—*presto!*—into the rightful owner and captain of your ship, even make you into an official adult. So shower up, make yourself a sandwich, go swimming. Do what you like for an hour."

I smiled in great relief. I would love that shower! I'd love all the things he offered.

"Peter won't mind?"

"Who?"

"Peter Vunderweer?"

"Oh! *Grandfather* Vunderweer! He's not even here; he's in the hospital. Nothing serious. Up in Florida."

I'd thought Peter had no family. But then Peter Vunderweer's life was all rumor anyway. Not even my parents had actually met him. Of course if Nicholas was the grandson, that would explain everything. Perhaps the island really was his to sell!

"So," I said, gazing at the old man's portrait, his grizzled fair hair. "This summer blondness is a Dutch trait?"

His smile was quick and winsome. "Exactly."

The shower was hot, powerful, and I stayed in it longer than my conscience said I should. Such a waste of fresh water! The soap smelled of rosemary and the towels were sumptuously heavy and white.

In his guest room, he had put out a long caftan for me, a presumptuous gesture, but then I glanced at the salt-stiff clothes I'd taken off.

The caftan looked new, but when I lifted it, I was aware of a clean grassy fragrance. I envisioned freshly cut meadows. Rain. I supposed it was kept for visitors. I stared at the blue dolphins that leaped around the hemline and surprised myself by slipping its silky fabric over my bare body. It felt like whispers, like water itself.

I stood motionless, hands deep in slits of pocket. I remembered the feel of tumbling through water with my dear boy-dolphin and how he had rescued me from loneliness, for a few days.

With a sad shake of my head, I dropped my pocketknife and remaining cash into the caftan's pockets, then rolled my dirty clothes in a towel and tucked them in a corner.

I looked at myself in the long mirror. My face had the same strong bones as Mother's. Same large auburn eyes and level brows. My breasts were prominent under the caftan's thin material, and you could see the long outline of my legs. I saw nothing of my father in me, although I felt he was inside. A gentler person than Mother, more tolerant.

I pushed back the damp fringes of my hair. I was a tall, slender young woman now, I could see that. I was good to look at.

In the refrigerator was a tempting bowl of fruit salad, which I ate standing up. Nicholas ran a fine household: clean, orderly, gracious.

He worked on my documents behind closed doors. I didn't wish to disturb him, so I settled into the hammock on the front porch, swaying as I watched the waves come in. The black yacht moved in sleepy half-circles around its anchor chain. The work was taking much longer than an hour. . . . I drowsed into a deep contented slumber.

I woke to a breeze-soft touch. Nicholas was bent over me, placing the gentlest of kisses on my forehead.

"Wake up, Sleeping Beauty. Your prince bears gifts."

He straightened and before I could even think about what had just happened, he held out a stack of gleaming new documents.

"I threw in a few extra things, citizenship papers for the United States as well as Great Britain, always good to have, and a letter from Yale University saying you're a grad student on an environmental mission—that's better than a ticket to Disneyland around here."

I paged through the authentic-looking documents, then spoke solemnly. "Thank you, Nicholas."

In truth the papers felt like a great weight in my hands. I sensed the terrible price of falseness and vowed to throw everything overboard once I was back on the boat—except the documents of boat ownership.

I promised myself that as soon as I turned eighteen—only months from now—I would replace everything with legitimate papers. I didn't care to be bad. Only to be free.

Still, Nicholas had only done as I asked of him, and he had done it swiftly and fairly. He gave me his hand and we walked onto the beach. A splendid sunset colored the air. The sky billowed with broken rows of cloudlets, radiating like waves from the disappearing point of sun. The bands intensified from pink to orange to yellow, became layered with lavenders and indigos.

I had never seen such a thing in all my life, and I was born beneath tropical skies. The cloud-waves throbbed over us, changing the sea and the sand into a shifting magical kingdom. Neither of us said a word. We dropped to our knees, rolled over on our backs, and watched. We barely breathed, knowing that all over the Caribbean, life was stopping for this sunset. We held hands: All that anchored us to this world was the touch of another human being.

And then as quickly as the day gave away its color, the night stole it back: purple, blue, gray . . . and it was gone. I let out a deep sigh. Nicholas raised on his elbow, turned to cup my cheek in his hand.

"So beautiful," he murmured, and moved to me as gently, as steadfastly, as a wave upon the shore.

His kiss was intense, tender, shifting.

The miraculous sunset, my first kiss, melded into one exquisite sensation.

I was overwhelmed.

o o o

Unexpectedly, Nicholas leaned back. His voice was as jubilant as if he'd won a great competition.

"This calls for another glass of wine—make that champagne! Hors d'oeuvres, the best Chez Nicholas has to offer!"

He kissed me lightly and was up and into the house. A light went on inside, a cozy light that showed him moving to his tasks, singing to himself. I was being roused in ways I couldn't understand.

And then he was returning through the dusk. He lowered a tray we both ignored, knelt to kiss me again.

I kissed him back, kissed him until I found myself lost. When I pulled back, needing to breathe, to share words, he would not let go. His body was suddenly rigid, his kiss now rough and demanding.

"No," I murmured. "Not so much, please."

"Not so much, please," he mocked viciously.

I was so shocked by his tone, I was slow to resist as he pinned me under him. His kiss became savage. My breath was being stolen from my body!

I was not accustomed to being forced. Mother's whole life had been dedicated to disallowing such things.

We struggled fiercely. I was greatly disadvantaged: lying

solidly beneath him in the deep sand, my legs fettered by the dress. He laughed as I wrenched my wrists from his grip.

"Now I suppose you'll go for that knife you carry with you. Did you think I didn't see it in those skimpy jean shorts of yours?"

His powers of observation were bizarrely keen; I saw that now. I saw danger where I could not have imagined it a few minutes before.

"And now your knife's right *here,* isn't it?"

He groped, finding it inside the pocket of the caftan, which had twisted and tucked between my thighs. He yanked the wads of fabric above my waist. I of course wore nothing beneath—my soiled clothes were still on his bathroom floor. Forgetting the knife, he shoved his hand between my legs.

Oona! Help me!

For once, she did not pause before responding. Her outrage was instant; Viking strength surged through my limbs. I threw Nicholas off and jumped to my feet, sand spilling whitely in the dusk.

He was instantly up and facing me. "Go ahead, use your knife, Bucky," he said softly. "You're perfect, you know. Feisty. You'll fit right into my princess collection. Go on . . ." His voice was hypnotic. "Get your knife, see what you can do before I take it away from you—"

So much talk about my knife! My leg snapped out from the tangle of fabric and struck him exuberantly in the abdomen. His eyes popped in surprise, and then he was down.

He writhed in the sand, fought to breathe. He would be

unable to rise for a moment; I had no need to strike him again. I shrugged out of the imprisoning dress, plucked my pocketknife and a handful of money from its pocket, grabbed the new documents, and raced for the dock. I gave no thought to covering myself or returning to his house for my clothes.

I swerved to avoid a box the size of a double coffin, then jumped into his motorboat. With a slice of my knife, I disabled its starter cord.

Nicholas was up and racing across the beach for me, his movement smooth and low as a panther's.

I scrambled aboard the *Svanhild* and raised her sails. Nicholas's fury was as real as the harsh twist of rope between my hands. I watched from the helm as he kicked at his motorboat, then straightened to stare out at me.

I stood tall and undaunted as the sails filled tightly and swept us across the inlet. Starlight glazed my bare skin with silver, and I saw myself as he did: the bold glistening figure of a woman he assumed he'd conquered. Sailing out of his life.

chapter

Birdie

icholas didn't come for me until the next morning. He was in a bad mood, but not as bad as I was.

Yesterday a helicopter landed here, surely to rescue me—and then flew away without me! I'd screamed until my throat ached and my lungs tightened. Then I called on the walkie-talkie, thinking the soldiers—the Australian marines?—might hear me, but they never even went inside. They looked down at a piece of paper, checked Nicholas over, then saluted him like he was their commander!

I didn't understand! Why hadn't they arrested him? I knew he appeared very different than my parents would have described, but surely they would look around just to be sure?

After they flew off, I was too depressed to move. I laid my head down on the table and tried not to dwell on my hoarse breathing. It was the rocking of the boat that finally roused me: the unmistakable wake of a passing boat. The Aussie marines were back!

I sprang to the porthole, instantly erasing all bad thoughts about them. Instead, it was a white sailboat, a pretty boat steered by a pretty girl. They whizzed straight past me. I couldn't shout anymore, my lungs were already suffering, but I pounded on the window until my fists and forearms were bruised up and down.

Of course even if the girl had been listening, she never would have heard the muffled thumping. All I could do was move to the other side of the boat, watch her tie up at the dock. She disappeared inside the house as though she belonged there.

It was still the afternoon, but I was completely worn out. I slept until a powerful orange light poured through the portholes, waking me as the entire depths of the boat turned pink-gold. Looking out, I saw a flaming sunset fan across the sky. Beneath it, two people kissed and rolled around the beach. Nicholas and the girl, of course. That such a thing could be happening right there in front of me, that they were so unaware of me or so uncaring that I watched, uncaring that I suffered, made me furious. I had no voice left for shouting. There was nothing to break. Nothing even to hurl around, except the huge sofa cushions.

I wrenched one free, tried to heave it. But it was too big and floppy. It fell heavily to the floor. I dropped onto it and had another kicking tantrum. It was like I was three years old and had been put in my room for something I completely didn't do.

By the time I finally pulled myself together, night was falling. I could still make out old Nicholas though, curled up there on the beach, *napping*. I knew people did that after having sex. And to confirm my suspicions, the girl was now completely naked. She rushed around in her long grown-up body, gleaming in the dusk like she was made of bronze. She was even curvier than Kirin! I was getting mad all over again! Was that her Le Cosmétique case in Nicholas's art room? I didn't know if I was jealous—it's not like Nicholas was my *boyfriend,* that would just be weird—or if this was just more information than I wanted. Did no one care that I was only thirteen years old?

I made myself leave the window and go to my berth. All I knew was that afternoon the soldiers had come and gone. The rest of what was happening out there had nothing to do with me.

o o o

When I woke up in the middle of the night, the girl's white boat was gone.

On shore, insects shrilled like police whistles. The moon was almost full. Its sharp-shadowed light picked out each blade of sea grass stiffly circling the house. A sudden movement brought my attention to the dock. Bajo! Bent double inside the motorboat, elbows jigging up and down as though he was working on the engine.

But in the middle of the night? By moonlight?

The lunatic scene, the maddening events of the last days left me so agitated, I couldn't go back to sleep.

I roughly booted up the Mac. A cartoon cat appeared above the start-up icons and gave a pixilated wave. "Hello, Penelope!" it said in a chipper electronic voice. "Have a nice day!" And then it was replaced by a bubbly screen saver.

Penelope? This wasn't even Nicholas's computer! Was it

Penelope's Le Cosmétique makeup case? Or was the Mac a souvenir from yet another girl Nicholas had stolen?

I had to get myself rescued!

I stayed up till dawn trying to figure out the Internet password. If I could get on the Internet, I could write for help. I typed in: *cheater, nicholas, nicky, naughty, naughtynicky, vunderweer, underwear.* A million other words. I just couldn't get it

I curled up on the velvet sofa, wrapped my arms around the same big cushion I'd been kicking, and sobbed. I was so lonely and afraid! I tried to pretend I was Kirin. If she'd survived, maybe I could too.

What was her secret?

I remembered her words just as I fell asleep: *The way I stay brave is by pretending I'm you, Birdie.*

○ ○ ○

I was still asleep when Nicholas barged in the next morning. My arms were still fastened around the cushion. My first waking breath told me my lungs were congested.

"Get up," he said. "Let me see what you've written."

"I need my inhaler."

"You need a lot of things. I'm pretty sick of girls *needing* things. What about my needs? Let me see what you wrote."

He stared at Penelope's orange Mac. Its blank monitor stared back.

"I didn't write anything," I croaked groggily. "I—"

"Stupid wench." He slammed the door, locked it, motored off.

Now I'd be stuck here at least until dinnertime! I heard myself wheezing. I had to calm down if I didn't want to end up dead from asthma.

I dragged myself over to a porthole and peered out. I couldn't believe my eyes. There was Mom's favorite caftan, her new dolphin dress, waving from a post like a flag. What else had Nicholas secreted away? Everything here was sneakiness and lies and nothing the way it seemed. It was just too much.

My chest tightened with each new thought. Poor Mom, her dream year stolen by Nicholas, her heart breaking at this very moment, not knowing where her daughter was. My parents' lives had been ruined by someone who thought of himself as naughty.

Lying down made breathing harder. I sat at the stupid Mac, leaned over it, and burst into tears. Stupid, I told myself. You're making yourself sicker. My words didn't help. Giant tears arced onto the keyboard as if they had a story of their own to tell.

I was miserable.

I drank eleven Pepsis, each one making me thirstier than the last. Hadn't Nicholas heard that people needed plain water? As usual, he'd turned the water off. Even if I could break into the storage tanks, a person could use stored water only for washing unless it was boiled. And of course, he'd turned off the fuel supply to the stove.

The story Nicholas had told me about the puppy and tumors coming out its ears was no doubt just that, a story, but I knew about bacteria and that a person could get really sick from bad food or water. Still, how nice it would be to take a cooling shower!

A stale can of Aquarium would have been heaven. . . .

I tried not to think about it anymore.

Which wasn't easy because it was roasting down here! I had the only fan in the main cabin going, but it was just a big noise and a pitiful warm breeze. I called Nicholas on the walkie-talkie. If the not-calling rule was still in effect, I was willing to take the consequences. Anything to get out of this heat and get my medication!

He didn't answer.

Bajo was back on the dock, this time banging around on a giant wooden crate. Tipped over on its side like that, it looked about five feet tall and seven feet long. Probably one of Nicholas's oversized refrigerators had come in it.

Fancy steel refrigerators, packed full as a grocery store. Every kind of cold tasty drink you could imagine, all for mean old stingy wicked Nicholas.

I thought about spending a few minutes shouting to Bajo for help, but what was the use of losing my voice to a person who couldn't hear and maybe or maybe not cooked cats?

I knew I had to finish Nicholas's story or I'd never get out of here. But writing on the Mac was not the same as fooling around trying to find the password. Sentences juggled nauseatingly in front of my eyes, and I was instantly reminded of how horrible it was to be seasick. I opened my journal and went back to working the old-fashioned way.

I worked until I finished the story, then read it over. The hero was no way Nicholas, but I was sure it would pass for how Nicholas saw himself. I'd told the story my way, and it had come out pretty well!

I chose a new page and wrote about twenty times, "Birdie rules! Nicholas sucks!" I felt better. My breathing eased and so did my anxieties. I flopped my journal on the table, wondering what I'd do for the rest of the day.

For the next hour I went back to guessing at the Mac's password, then drowned my failure with the final Pepsi. The last of my clothes were drenched with sweat, so I peeled down to underpants. I couldn't eat anything, at least not the gruesome canned stuff Nicholas kept on the boat: Spam, greasy corned beef hash, cold tamales. For a while I just stood there looking out the porthole, wondering where that girl, or lady, had come from.

Was she Penelope?

My ears never stopped listening for helicopters.

When the sun went down, I tried prying open the hatch, the portholes, hoping not so much to get out as to let some air in. I saw the palms moving on shore, almost felt their cooling breeze, but none of it made it past my imagination and into the boat.

The first star winked above the island, and I wished on it. A hopeless, childish thing to do, but wishes were all I had left.

Calista was far behind me. As soon as I was able to leave the sails unattended, I went below to put clothes on. I chose my best, a well-used but clean pair of linen trousers and a linen shirt, in two different shades of no special color.

At the wheel, in the soft midnight darkness, the fabric flapped lightly around me. In my sensitized state, I felt everything. I thought about Nicholas and our first kiss, and what happened afterward. It was like I'd spent the day with two different people. *He's a bad person,* said my brain. *A disordered personality at the least.* But part of me kept returning to that kiss, Nicholas so beautiful, his smooth muscular body pushing up against mine.

"Stop!" I said out loud. I didn't want these thoughts!

Oona?

Will you help me?

You must listen to your rational self, or you also will become two people.

I nodded. Suddenly exhausted, I bedded down on deck. As I

slept, my thoughts became clear, clearer than today's crystal glass of wine.

O O O

I awoke as abruptly as if Oona had pinched me. The moon loomed roundly overhead, its mouth open in a silent scream, its halo silver as pinned-up braids. My heart beat loudly and the stars blinked accusing eyes.

Of course that had been the *Engelberta* in Calista's bay. I'm not wrong about such things!

Why had I not insisted that Nicholas explain? Had I been so smitten with him I'd turned away from knowing the truth? About the *Engelberta,* and about his character? Was he just a shyster, a naughty boy who grew rich on forged papers? Or someone who stole boats? Not a small thing! Or worse, a true pirate, who would take anything by any means—even lives—if it added treasure to his trove.

The stack of forged documents gleamed in the moonlight, their edges fluttering as if trying to escape the anchoring weight I'd set on top of them. Until now the prisons I'd feared had been in my mind. These false papers had turned my cherished *Svanhild* into a prison that was suddenly real.

I crumpled each paper and fed it to the sea. I left nothing to save myself from foes that lived in the future, or in my imagination.

Dawn broke, but its soft pink light did not calm my anxieties. What if the old German couple were prisoners aboard the

Engelberta? And if they weren't, where were they? And Peter Vunderweer? Was he really in Florida, or was everything a lie?

I knew the codes of the sea and abided by them. They were simple and had nothing to do with fickle land laws that changed at each new harbor. My papers had to do with land laws. A stolen boat had to do with the code of the sea. If an elderly German couple had been forcibly separated from their boat, or from their lives, it was piracy.

I brought the *Svanhild* about, wrestled with her as the sails lost the wind. The rigging, its metal holdings and line, went slack and clanged loudly against each other and the masts. I hauled at the wheel, and the sails snapped taut as we pointed back where we'd come from.

The night turned hotter than any sauna. I sweated myself dry; my tongue seemed Velcroed to the roof of my mouth and my eyeballs felt scraped by their lids. I fell asleep, woke violently at dawn dreaming that Nicholas held me underwater. I sat up feeling suffocated—my asthma was so much worse! I gasped, panicked by how little air I could take in.

I tried to be positive, to remember that suffering such as this was important to my writing, to my book. But in my heart, I doubted there'd be a book, or a future at all. I wanted to call Nicholas right now, to beg him for help, but I didn't want to wake him up. I'd written this down so I'd remember: *mad = bad*.

I waited, thinking calm thoughts, imagining Dad and me down in the cool basement, watering my special lettuce. I dragged myself to the shower, opened the faucet and was rewarded by a single splash of coolness. I turned my face to the remaining drip, mouth and eyes closed, savoring the heavenly wetness of my hair.

And then I was too weak to stand any longer. I flopped on the floor next to the table, waited patiently until pink light streamed palely through the porthole and across my thin legs. Surely he was up now, having his fresh-ground coffee. I carefully pulled myself to my feet, made my way to the walkie-talkie.

The words were thick in my mouth.

"Bir—um, Bugs to Nicholas, Bugs to Nicholas, over."

I called exactly the way Nicholas had taught me. I wanted it to be clear that I was following the rules. He had to come! I had to have my inhaler!

I was faint from the incredible heat; even my heart felt hot as it raced weakly inside my chest. I needed one of Dr. Bennett's wonder shots that left me nervous but breathing freely.

I needed my parents.

"Nicholas . . . Nicholas . . . please?" I abandoned protocol for begging. "I have your story. . . . It's finished. Can you come here? I'll read it to you . . . please?" My voice quavered. "Over."

The walkie-talkie crackled.

"Sure, Bugs, be right there! *Please* is the magic word. Hey! We should take a swim! It's hot as the Fourth of July—hey!—it *is* the Fourth of July! See you in a jiff."

The Fourth of July! I'd thought we were past that! Had I miscounted? I pulled my journal out from under a pile of my dirty clothes, counted out loud. Each mark was a day filled with fear and anxiety. But each one proof that I was still here. My count was right. If it was the Fourth of July, it meant that the days when I was drugged must have been fewer than I'd imagined. Or else Nicholas was just lying about the date.

He didn't come for what seemed like hours. He was *showing* me. Finally, I felt the sway of the boat as he hopped on board.

Fresh air flooded into the cabin. I staggered forward, reaching up the stairs for him as if he were Santa Claus.

Saint Nicholas, Dad had mockingly called him. He'd seen Nicholas for what he was, he'd *known* . . .

"Uh-oh," Nicholas said. "Who's got the wheezie-beezies?"

His muscles were slick with suntan oil, and he wore only swimming trunks. Baggy trunks that looked new. That bright Hawaiian pattern was so unlike him . . . it was more like . . . Dad! Those were *Dad's* trunks—

Outrage burst in me like an H-bomb. *H* for *hate*! I opened my mouth, but there was no extra breath for words.

He stepped down the companionway, gasped at the heat.

"Whoa, Bugs, you shouldn't let it get so stuffy down here. Come on now, you need a swim. We'll celebrate the Fourth with a picnic, two American citizens, at least one of them celebrating their independence. . . . . Laugh, Bugs, that was a joke."

I sagged against the wall.

He said, "Uh-oh," and slipped the inhaler from his pocket. He gently supported me as he held it to my lips.

"That's a girl." He squeezed mist into my mouth, watched me pant to get a little inside me. "Why did you wait so long? All you had to do was ask Naughty Nick. I'm here for you, Bugsy."

I tried to check my scowl, but he saw it. His eyes went cold and he let go of the inhaler.

"Do it yourself, then," he said.

I slid to the floor, and he turned away from me.

It was apparently, once again, 100% up to me to stay alive. I clutched at the inhaler, squeezing, hitching in mist, squeezing, hitching.

Nicholas casually rooted through the clothes on the table. His voice cheerful and light again, scolding me for being so messy.

His mood changes were getting more rapid, more unpredictable.

I shook the inhaler. So little left. I had to be very careful—what would happen when it was gone? As he folded my clothes, I slipped it into my pocket.

"Ah-ha!" Nicholas said, finding my journal. "*The Adventures of Naughty Nicholas!* Let's get to it!"

My heart nearly stopped. It was the first time Nicholas had ever picked it up.

"Uh-uh, Nicholas," I croaked. "Private, remember."

"Yeah, right. Our *rule*. Seems like our rules are getting bent to hell lately."

Had he ever respected the privacy of my journal? I suddenly saw what a joke that was. This was Nicholas's kingdom. Rules were for me, not him! Why hadn't I just torn his story out? I'd planned to! Now my words—all those *Nicholas sucks!*—were going to fry me!

He pulled me to my feet, pushed me ahead of him onto the deck.

"Let the Fourth of July festivities begin." His voice sounded exactly like I felt: flattened as the bottom of the sea.

"It's not the Fourth of July," I said dully. I was so sick of his lies. He'd never even named the boat after me, the way he'd promised! "The Fourth of July is over."

"Whatever." He stepped heavily into the motorboat. "Merry Christmas, if that's what you want to hear. See you on shore."

I watched him take off alone across the cove. If he thought I'd swim after him—that I *could*!—he was nuts. Didn't he see I was half dead? I leaned against the mast, glaring at him until he finally caught on and turned his boat around.

In those two minutes, he had gone completely back to cheerful. "Okay, party pooper, hop in. I'll be your chauffeur." He stuck his fingers into my limp hair and ruffled it way too hard. "Needy little pill bug."

At the dock, Bajo seemed to have abandoned the crate, a moldered thing that looked unworthy of repair. It reminded me of the mossy playhouse in my backyard, where Kirin and I became closer than close—except this didn't have any windows and wasn't really tall enough to stand up in.

Nicholas had set up a picnic on a blanket under a palm tree. I rushed to the thermos, poured a huge glassful of lemonade, and drank it down. I collapsed in the shade, reached for more. Nicholas lounged on his side, thumbed through my notebook.

Suddenly his head jerked up, eyes narrowed as he stared at me, then back at my journal. He turned a few more pages, paused, read some more.

"So, Birdwinkle Sidwell—"

His serious face—speaking my forbidden name out loud— made my heart stop. I touched the inhaler in my pocket. He saw.

"Give it here." I handed it over, and he returned to my journal. "Looks like we need to talk about this."

"You promised me, Nicholas, you said—"

"I promised, you promised, my rules, your rules, la dee-da dee-da!"

He'd flipped again, his voice suddenly loud and silly.

"Oh, look here, this is priceless!" He cleared his throat, read aloud, " 'I knew my beloved husband would now make me his wife, and that afterward we would nap comfortably together. . . .' " He yelped with delight. "Steamy stuff, Bugs! You're a budding romance writer!"

I was about to protest, but he'd already flipped forward to the page titled "Reasons Nicholas Might Have Kidnapped Me."

"Go ahead," he said without looking up. "Have some nachos, eat something, *Birdwinkle Sidwell*—the girl who doesn't care to be Princess of Calista—who lives in the past as though it were nicer than the present."

I shifted to take another gulp of lemonade, moved as carefully as if the beach were a thin crust of glass, ready to shatter under the weight of my mistakes.

"Nicholas?" The last thing I ought to do was ask him this question, but I had to. "I don't understand why you took me. . . . Why did you?"

He cocked his head in an exaggerated way. "Well, I sure don't know, Bugs. Maybe 'cause you were just so stinking cute. Or maybe because I'm collecting princesses and I thought you'd look good on the shelf." He shrugged. "Only now I'm thinking you'd look better in a *drawer,* some dark drawer that never gets opened up again."

Why had I asked? *Mad = bad!*

"Anyhoo!" He was having fun with this. "*I* don't know why I took you, but *you* seem to have some ideas on the subject. Let's start at the bottom of your list—" He winked up at me. "Work our way up."

My hand shook as I balanced my glass on the sand, stared at it, at the thermos, anywhere but Nicholas's face.

"Let's see here, number four: because you'll be beautiful in ten years? And I'm supposed to be waiting for that?"

I noticed that the thermos was wrapped in used computer paper, to keep it cool. It was the printout of the front page of a newspaper.

"You're already beautiful, Princess, I've told you that." He shook his head sadly. "Let's move on. Number three: because I'm lonely and need company?" He nodded. "Very sensitive, Birdwinkle. Yes, of course one who lives alone on an island *does* get a tad lonely, and one does need company."

The newspaper's heading read *The Daily Herald;* that could be anywhere.

"Number two: Because I'm weird."

He spoke each word carefully, leaving ominous spaces between.

"*Weird,* Birdwinkle? Compared to *what*? I'd never seen anyone more ready than you to be rescued from an ordinary life. . . ."

The print was small underneath the newspaper's banner. I poured another glass, squinted at it: *3 July—Sint Maarten, N.A.*

St. Maarten, Netherland Antilles! Could that be where we were? Right where we started? Not in the Cook Islands, but still in the Caribbean!

Why else would he print out such a newspaper, if it weren't the local news? He wouldn't!

Nicholas said, "Do you think the *mailman* would have bothered providing all this for you?"

What was he talking about? I had to find a way to let someone know where we were!

"And now the winner! Since you seem to need a reason, I vote for number one! Getting *money* for old Birdwinkle, ex-princess of Calista! That makes *sense,* Bugs, even to weird old Naughty Nick!"

He was going to punish me big-time. How could I have been so stupid as to write this stuff down? He might punish me to death! I had to get off Calista—

We jerked our heads skyward, hearing the sound at the exact same moment. Not a helicopter, but the drone of an airplane engine! I saw it there on the horizon, no doubt the soldiers coming back—the real coast guard all along—armed and ready to drop troops.

Nicholas stared hard. He was way too cool to show alarm.

It slowly drew close: a rickety little advertising plane, its bright red-white-and-blue banner waving behind.

HAPPY FORT JULY TO AMERICANS! BUY FROM MR. SUN-GLASSES!!!!

It *was* the Fourth! The pilot probably couldn't even see us down here. He flew on past, headed for bigger islands, places where happy-go-lucky sun-blinded Americans celebrated their independence.

My voice was small inside the silence. "Was that helicopter here for me, Nicholas? Yesterday? Why didn't they search? *Why?*" I knew I sounded like a tearful little baby.

He lifted my chin with a gentle finger. "Oh, Bugs, haven't you gotten it? It's all about cheating. They were looking for some dude with dark eyes and a mondo scar on his face. And why would a rich guy like me kidnap someone anyway? A little show of wealth, and poof! suddenly the law disappears. Cops and soldiers are no different than anyone else. I'm rich, Bugs, look around; no one messes with money!"

I nodded. Even on TV, the police never tore apart mansions to look for drugs or kidnapped children.

"And I'm about to be richer. What's the old homestead worth back in River City, oops, Riverton? Two hundred thousand? Everyone's house is worth at least that anymore. Three hundred? How much in the bank? They'd have a fat college fund for their one-and-only, right? Join in here, Bugs, help me out. What are you worth, half a mil . . . more? Every dollar helps . . ." He smiled, counting the money in his head. "I'll let you write the ransom note yourself, my authoress of the future." He glanced at the journal. "Isn't that what you call yourself?"

"Is Peter Vunderweer your real grandpa or did you kill him? And who are *Mueti* and *Papi,* from the boat . . . Did you kill *them*? Are you going to kill *me*?"

"Oh, Bugs, it would have been so nice to have you on Calista.

That other stuff was just business. I took you because I wanted you. You were a keeper; why did you have to spoil things? Why am I such a sucker for clever girls?" He gave a small slap to either side of his face, pretending to beat himself up.

Then suddenly all pretense was gone. "In the end you're all a *pain in the ass!*"

He jerked me to my feet, shoved my journal into my hands, headed us back to the motorboat. "I don't like your story's ending, Birdwinkle. I haven't even read it and I don't like it. Fix it, get it right before dark."

On deck he unlocked the bilge, reached to wrench the water lever into working position.

"I'm having a little going-away party for you, Birdie Sidwell. You're moving into your new home-away-from-home—a little something Bajo's making up for you."

He pushed me inside the sailboat, then spoke through the locked door. "You smell bad. Take a shower. Drink the water if you want. It doesn't matter."

Didn't matter if I drank it because I was going to die anyway?

As I heard his boat motor away I turned in little circles, trying to keep from going into shock.

If Nicholas actually planned to keep me in that box on the dock, I really might die. Was that the plan? Lots of kidnappers let their victims die!

No! I told myself. *You can't drown a Duck!*

I wouldn't panic. My lungs were clear and I needed to keep my mind that way—

Suddenly a remarkable idea came to me. What I needed was a bath! Nothing on earth calmed me quicker, or made me sharper!

There was actually a sort of bathtub available. The boat's fiberglass shower stall had a deep lip around it, up to my calves, either to keep water from spilling out, or maybe even meant for this, the occasional luxury bath.

I covered the drain and let the shower run until its bottom filled up. I swished in a little shampoo for bubbles and got in. Warm. I leaned back, not caring that water sloshed over the edge.

A bath is nothing like a shower or a swim or anything else. I felt the familiar transporting of my mind and began to drift. I had time. I didn't need to think up a new story for Nicholas. He'd love what I'd already written. I closed my eyes.

When I opened them again, I'd lost all track of time. All I knew was my fingers were pruney and the bubbles were long gone. I held my breath and sank below the surface.

Nicholas's words floated across my mind, clear as the airplane's banner:

No one messes with money.

Money! I leaped from the bath and ran for the Mac. I typed in *m-o-n-e-y*. With a small musical crescendo, the Internet opened up like the universe.

chapter
20

MORGAN

Something was up.

By twilight, seven different helicopters had passed overhead. None even bothered coming for a closer look at me. They weren't looking for anything small—a lost fishing boat or a man overboard—they traveled far too hastily for that. They were searching for the kidnapped girl!

Questions were building up, and so was my anxiety.

Twice I scurried up the mast, checking the horizon for anything unusual, or even anything familiar. There was nothing to be seen, no ships, no islands, not even a bird.

We were still hours from Calista. It seemed the greater my sense of urgency, the more the winds slackened. It was particularly hot, the going heavy. I felt as though we were pushing through something other than air. It was almost as if an invisible cloud of evil had lowered onto the sea, and only my strength of will could move us through it.

chapter 21

Birdie

I dripped bathwater all over the floor as I stood there, figuring out the e-mail program. The sun wasn't setting yet, but I had no idea how long I'd been in the tub. I'd start with a group mailing of all the e-mail addresses I knew by heart: hsidwell@usgov.org, superintendent@rivertonschools.org, kiriniskool-@aol.com, soccersamantha@northwest.net, madmax@northwest.net, fans@courtneystarz.com, customerservice@gap.com . . .

I didn't really know that many. I'd have to look up the police in St. Maarten, the police in Riverton, the coast guard. I doubted the president would be listed.

There wasn't a minute to waste. I tabbed down to the subject line, typed *RESCUE ME,* tabbed to the message box. My fingers flew across the keys.

```
I am alive! I'm on a little island called
Calista in the Caribbean, close to St.
Maarten.
I'm on a different boat than you saw, a
black boat this time, with its name
```

```
covered over with tape. It's parked out in
Calista's bay. Nicholas is not Australian.
His last name may be Vunderweer. The coast
guard was here yesterday, but they didn't
even bother looking around for me!
```

No—too upsetting! Mom and Dad probably couldn't take much more than they'd already been through. I backspaced, re-typed the sentence:

```
The coast guard was here yesterday but
didn't find me.
```

I swallowed hard, thinking of this e-mail suddenly appearing in front of my parents—but this was no time to fall apart. I typed,

```
I'm not hurt—
```

I heard the motorboat start up and frantically added,

```
Come quick.
```

I ran to the window.
Nicholas was halfway here!
I'd wanted to mention the *crate,* and to tell everyone to be sure not to write back—Nicholas would get their e-mails on his

other computers—but there was no time. I hadn't even said who I was!

I typed in *Birdie Sidwell* and hit Send—but I'd paused too long and been disconnected. I retyped *m-o-n-e-y*!

Nicholas called out cheerfully from the deck, as if nothing had happened earlier, "Let's get back to the house, Bugs—it's party time! I've got big Bob and the Wailers going, the chicken's fried up, and I'm lonesome without you—"

He opened the hatch. I jumped away from the computer and screamed.

"Whoa, Bugs—you're all naked, Princess!" He cocked his head, a little smile on his face.

I yelled, "For Pete's sake, Nicholas! Let me get dressed!" and shoved the hatch closed.

I reached over to the computer and hit Send . . . sending, sending, *sent*. . . . I clicked Disconnect, dragged down the Special menu, clicked Sleep. The monitor went innocently black.

My clothes were damp and horrible to put back on. And Nicholas was right, they did smell bad! I had no choice but to pull them on and stomp up the stairs.

Nicholas had a weird look on his face. He reached to put his arm around me. "My little princess is growing up."

Something about that look was scarier than the idea of being put into a box.

"Nicholas." I flapped my journal at him like I was shooing a fly. "You're going to love the new ending."

He followed me into the motorboat like a puppy.

Bajo was back on the dock, banging on my wooden prison with the handle of his machete, making no improvement whatsoever. As Nicholas had pointed out, he *was* a crappy carpenter. He scowled as he worked. I'd never seen him not scowling. Maybe that was his normal face. He never looked up at us, and Nicholas never looked over at him, or even acknowledged that he was there, or that a crate was being made for me, his bad puppy!

I was clearly the only noncrazy person on Calista.

The crate was way too big to pick up and move, but way, way too little to keep a normal human being in for any time! My chest began to tighten, and I forced myself to think about other things. Maybe it wouldn't even happen! Nicholas was in a great mood, and he was now calling this evening a *date,* not a *going-away* party.

He frowned at my dirty clothes, sent me for a shower. A clean outfit was waiting for me when I got out. He'd picked one of my nice little halter tops and the long flowing scarf I used as a wraparound skirt.

Alone in the guest room, I caught my reflection in the mirror. I didn't look as scared as I felt. In fact I looked nice. My hair fell over my shoulders. I saw, from the way the halter fit, that my bust had blossomed in the tropical climate. I froze. Nicholas had seen me undressed! At the time he'd barged in, I'd been frantically trying to send the e-mail—too frantic for that rather enormous event to register!

I blushed hotly, pulled my pink-and-orange vest on over the

skimpy halter, and patted the generous pockets. Each flatly covered either side of my chest; I was back to looking like a kid.

Nicholas had set up a table on the front porch. A platter of his fried chicken was carefully arranged there, along with wineglasses and candles.

"Take off the vest, Princess," he said in a neutral voice. "It's hot this evening."

"No," I said, keeping my voice as neutral as his. "I could get asthma again. Mmm. Chicken smells fabulous."

Actually, it did. I was starved; I couldn't even remember when I'd last eaten. He held out a chair for me, sat down himself. The sun was going down. Steel drum music bonked out from the CD player and the palm trees rustled. I could relax now, just keep things stable until my e-mails bounced through the airways and landed—hopefully—in the right places.

I wolfed down two drumsticks, then felt slightly sick to my stomach. I wondered how it would go once the coast guard landed. I figured by the time my e-mail was passed on to them and they flew here from Puerto Rico or wherever they were based, it'd be really late. A midnight sting. They probably had a code name for the mission by now, something like Operation Birdsong.

As night began to fall, I read Nicholas his story. It took a long time, and I finished it by candlelight. I'd used real dialogue in it, and I read those parts with expression. When I closed my journal, there was a moment of silence. Nicholas's face floated above the romantic glow of candles. His blue eyes were gentle and dreamy. Why did he have to be so bad?

He gently applauded, then looked deep into my eyes.

"Princess, you have completely captured the real Nicholas in prose. The *real* me, the hero. I am so touched."

I suddenly feared having given him too much.

In fact, I'd given him everything! I had nothing left to make me valuable to keep around.

"There's more, Nicholas! Wait till tomorrow when you hear the rest! A special surprise ending—"

"You gave me the ending, Bugs—it was perfect."

"Great, but not perfect. There's an *epilogue,* the after-story, and it *is* perfect—even more exciting than you becoming the richest man on earth. . . ."

His eyes glistened with interest. He put down his napkin, *hooked*—and then we heard the choppers coming. They were very far away, but it sounded like an army of them.

He quickly blew out the candles, turned out every light in the house. I slipped my journal under my vest. It was all I had left; I wasn't leaving it behind.

He took my hand, made me rush around with him. Suddenly he was all business.

"Sit down in the kitchen. Wait there. That means don't get up for a drink, don't go to the bathroom. Sit. Wait."

I sat. (Good puppy.) I planned to bolt as soon as he left the room, hide in the jungle until I was rescued.

But when he reached the door he paused and came back. He rummaged through a drawer for duct tape, tore strips of it to fasten my wrists and ankles to the chair. (Bad puppy.)

He'd never done anything like this before. All along, we'd pretended I was something more than a prisoner.

We were now totally on to each other.

The noise of the choppers came closer, backed off, closer again, and then they were gone. Pure silence. It was true night now, not a spark of light on the island. Maybe they couldn't do a midnight sting. Maybe they couldn't land in the dark on a tiny island—or even if they could, the rescue would have been too dangerous. I had to believe they'd be back first thing in the morning—dawn's early light, just like in "The Star-Spangled Banner"!

Nicholas went in and out of the kitchen several more times, carrying boxes of things. The screen door banged each time he left the house and returned. Then his flashlight sliced through the darkness and came to rest on me.

"Ho-kay, Bugs, here we go."

Ripping the tape off that way did not feel good, but I didn't make a sound, and he didn't apologize. Instead he grabbed my wrist hard and led me out to the crate.

My heart banged when I saw the bars on the crate's narrow door. He felt me squirm and used his soft puppy-training voice, "Shhh, shhh . . . now, now."

When he pushed me at the door, I tried to break away.

He said, "Sorry, Bugs," and he truly sounded like he was.

He tucked a tiny flashlight and my inhaler into my vest pockets, then handed me a pen. "For your journal," he said, glancing at my vest where I'd thought it was so invisibly hidden.

He was doing it again! Trying to make me feel grateful, when he was the one responsible for all my problems! He was like a genius at this!

He flashed his big flashlight around, showing me where I was. There was just enough height for me to stand up, and a little more than enough length to lie down. He'd stacked cases of Aquarium along one side, forming a water-can bench with my sleeping bag on top. There were bunches of green bananas hanging in one corner, and a box filled with snap-open canned foods, M&M's, plastic spoons, paperback books, bug spray, a rain poncho, a package of soap, a washcloth, Kleenex.

How long does he think I'll be in there?

He shined his light on a bucket hanging on the wall. "For the bathroom."

Then he clicked his flashlight off, padlocked the door, and vanished without a sound.

I didn't panic. I'd be rescued in the morning. Easy to find, right here on the dock.

. . . Why *had* Nicholas left me out here where they'd see me first thing? And why all the provisions? I didn't get it. I tried to hang on to my outrage, but water lapped quietly around the pilings and lulled me into a strangely peaceful mood. Like I was on a real camping trip. The box was positioned so the barred door faced the water. There was a breeze and I had a view straight into Cheater's Bay. This was a lot better than being on the boat.

I curled up on my water-can bed and looked out at the horizon. Zags of lightning flicked on and off, a long long way from here. There was always the possibility of rain on Calista, not the kind we used to have in Riverton, gentle and long lasting, but brief, wild storms, over before you knew it. A green plastic tarp drooped over the crate. Nicholas, of course, had thought of everything.

Except how to keep me from guessing his password! I smiled, feeling like Fat Silly when we used to put him in his cage to take him to the vet. He never minded, as long as we gave him his favorite blankie. I sighed and slipped inside my sleeping bag.

○ ○ ○

I woke to a slight sound, a muffled bump. The night was moonless, pitch-black. The wind was moving in, bringing the lightning closer. But that wasn't what woke me. I stared into the bay. Beyond our black boat was another boat. A white one, no more visible than a ghost. It was so close to the black boat, it must have been tied to it.

Another small bump, and a figure appeared on the black boat's deck, moved across it silent as a vampire. It disappeared down the companionway. The wind suddenly rattled the rigging against the mast as if it were a burglar alarm. I held my breath, hoping Nicholas wouldn't wake.

I waited for the figure to come back on deck. An image of James Bond jumped to mind. Silly, but a kind of giddiness was building inside me. So what if I suddenly felt like I was inside a movie? It was a movie with a good ending! I smiled in the dark, so excited I was about to pop! The rescue was finally happening!

I couldn't risk calling out, identifying myself. The house was too close and Nicholas might still be awake. Instead I grabbed my little flashlight and blinked it on-off, on-off, on-off.

I never even saw the figure come back up on deck or heard

his dinghy go into the water. He was almost to the dock before I caught the sound of oars swiftly skimming the water.

This guy was *good*!

He stealthily moved from the dinghy onto the dock and had almost reached my crate when my light caught him right in the face—

"Damn!" I said out loud, and lowered the light.

It wasn't a special agent at all! It was that *girl*! She'd put clothes on, but it was definitely the naked girl, back for more kissing!

I was ready to hurl a can of peaches at her when the lightning lit her face again. Her eyes were fixed on me in a steady, caring way.

I had just opened my mouth to say "Help me!" when Nicholas leaped from behind my crate and hit her on the head with his flashlight. She crumpled to the dock. Except for the soft crack, there hadn't been a sound.

Damn again! Obviously they'd broken up after the kissing—

The clouds bulged overhead, flickered with light. There was Bajo next to Nicholas, or had he been there all along? They were both dressed in dark clothes, quiet as a pair of rats.

So was I, until they pushed the girl into my cage.

"Birdie," Nicholas said. "*Oof* . . . meet Morgan."

"No!" I said, trying to push her back out. "There's no room!"

"Oh, Bugs." Nicholas was laughing softly. "It's wartime. In wartime, we have to make sacrifices."

Then the girl was there, a warm heap pressed against my legs. I shined my weak little flashlight on her face, and she suddenly became real to me. Her features were exotic, like a cat, that kind of cheekbones. But there was also something innocent about her.

She was seriously unconscious. No one slept with their neck cricked like that. And she had a giant lump on her head. Nicholas had really hurt her! I found myself furious with him all over again. I straightened her out the best I could and covered her with my sleeping bag.

Bajo was rowing her dinghy back to her boat. Nicholas was in his motorboat, heading for his own boat.

No sails were raised, no running lights turned on. Both sets of engines rumbled to life, both anchors clattered as they were brought up on deck. Then, black and white, the two ghosts drew away from Calista and disappeared.

○ ○ ○

I woke before dawn to the sound of Nicholas returning in his motorboat. The bay was dark and empty. The clouds boiled with unshed rain.

The girl was still asleep, her skin tinged blue in the storm-light.

Nicholas stopped for a brief peek.

"There's my girls."

"I hate you, Nicholas."

"No you don't. You love me. You'll be thinking about me the rest of your life—which come to think of it, might not be that long."

I scowled. "Why put all this food and stuff in here if you want us dead? You make no sense at all, Nicholas. You're totally insane!"

"Whatever," he said, shaking a can of spray paint. I choked on its fumes as he swooped it up and down the side of our crate.

"There . . ." he said, ". . . *Birdie* . . . and . . . *Mor* . . . *gan.* Your official coffin."

I gasped.

"Just kidding," he said. "I meant official *mailbox*—in case the postman wants to make a delivery." He gave the can a final squirt. "Seriously, though, Bugs, we've had our little problems, but we'll look back and laugh at all this."

He smiled at me. Even in the dim light, his teeth shone white and perfect.

"That was the soldiers buzzing us last night," he said. "You knew that, didn't you? They'll be back to pay us a little visit this morning. It's routine; they always double-check."

Always? How many times had he dealt with them?

The soldiers no doubt meant the U.S. Coast Guard, but he was giving away nothing.

He leaned close. "So here's how it's going to go: I'm going into the house now, see when they're due—easy as pie to find out if you're Naughty Nick. Then we'll do a little re-arranging."

The thunder rumbled so deeply the entire dock trembled. It felt like the morning had turned around and was headed back toward night.

"They'll look around a little more, check the house, maybe

the other shore; then they'll vamoose for good. They've got no reason to think you're here." He seemed calm and maddeningly sure of himself. "The provisioning is for just-in-case. You might have noticed, I'm a thorough kind of guy."

I tried to glare, but it was panic I felt.

He said, "That Aussie fellow on a motor yacht doesn't exist anymore. No one will put it together. Your case is about to close." He held out his shapely tan hand, closed it slowly to a fist. Then peered sympathetically at me. "Poor Bugs, you were thinking they'd find you." His hand shot between the bars, gave my hair a nasty jerk. "Not a chance. Not where you're going."

I grabbed at his arm, tried to scratch it, bite it, anything! But he was too quick.

My head spun with questions: Where *were* we going? And who was this girl—he'd said Morgan, not Penelope! What had happened to the boats? Why hadn't Bajo come back? And the biggest question, *What will happen to me?*

I didn't even bother asking. I just shook my head.

"That's right, Bugs. You'll never know."

The moment he disappeared into the house, lightning flashed overhead, knifed the clouds wide open. Bucketfuls of rain splashed noisily down on the tarp. That was the kind of luck Nicholas had, always too quick to get caught.

I sat on the bank of Aquarium cans, head in my hands, thinking over what he'd said. Was this really a routine check? I didn't think so—there were a *lot* of helicopters in the air the night before. But even if they were on to Nicholas, he had a plan. He always had a plan.

A shout came from the house. The screen door banged shut and he ducked through the rain to the dock.

He smacked his hand against the bars, right in front of my face.

"You shouldn't have done that, Birdwinkle—*bad, bad, bad*—now you'll see what happens to clever girls!"

He ran for the tractor, ready there on the dock.

My e-mail had gotten through! He'd no doubt seen it in the Sent mail—I'd had no time to delete it—or maybe Dad had written back?

Now we both knew: There would be nothing routine about this coast guard landing!

That quickly, the rain blew over. A sultry dull gray dawn was left behind, leaving plenty of light for the copters to land.

I thought I heard the roar of their engines, but it was only the tractor pulling close behind me.

Nicholas jumped off it, pitched the crate forward, back, big cracks opening and closing between boards, swearing as he wrestled us onto the tractor's front loader.

The girl murmured in her sleep.

"It's all right," I whispered. "Everything's all right."

I wasn't so sure about that as we were carted off into the jungle. The crate creaked and rattled with every bump, and vines snapped like the breaking of innocent necks.

chapter

22

MORGAN

I woke from a life of perfect freedom to find myself locked inside a lightless box.

I have a rational mind. It does no good to become enslaved to one's apprehensions. I've faced upending storms and the loss of two siblings and two parents without quailing. But how could I have imagined a thing such as this ahead of time, or prepared myself for it?

Hell is the thing you most fear. Without ever having put words to it, I'd found mine.

o o o

I opened my eyes but saw nothing. My head hurt very much. Another being pressed close to me. Such heat. A small wretched sound came from me.

It's all right.

"Then why can't I see, Oona? Why don't I know where I am?" I spoke out loud, for the comfort of hearing myself.

Oona answered immediately.

This isn't going to make any sense to you, okay? But you're in a box with me, underground.

You mean in the deep?

Well, in the ground, but not really deep.

We're dead then? Buried like land people?

Are you thirsty—don't! Don't try to jump up. It's really small in here!

Oona, I'm very afraid!

I'm not who you think . . . look.

A light suddenly lit Oona's face from underneath. I stifled a cry. With time, her hair had grown long and luxuriant. And, as to be expected from being in the deep, she was quite pale. It was a shock to me, having my sister appear under such circumstances. I wondered if the wine that Nicholas had given me contained a slow-acting hallucinogen.

Nicholas—the pirate. I remembered sailing to Calista to stop him and . . .

Oona said, "I want you to look around quick at where we are; I don't want to wear out my flashlight. See, here's water, stuff to eat. We pee, whatever, in the bucket. The main problem is no room, but if you feel like it, you could sit up here with me and that would work a lot better. I'm going to turn the light back off, okay?"

It was not okay at all! The dark made me want to run, to kick my way out of wherever I was. I tried to take in all the information. It hurt my head to move, but I was able to get untangled from my sister and push myself up onto a berth composed of cans.

Oona said, "Practice breathing deeply. That's saved my life more than once. We pretty much have to be calm, okay?"

We were sitting side by side now, as close as two people can be.

"I understand." I also began to understand that this child was very excitable. Oona was not excitable.

"The good news is the coast guard has landed here! I heard them come down just as we were dumped in the ground. It's just a matter of time before they force our location out of Nicholas. They have special forcing techniques."

"The coast guard." I was not fully understanding what she had said. Was this the girl they were looking for? The one Nicholas said was kidnapped?

I decided to be frank about my anxieties concerning the coast guard. "I understand the coast guard is here. I also understand that the coast guard is not always good."

"I totally thought that! The marines would be way better. The coast guard doesn't even wear camos, they have like mailman uniforms—"

I touched her tight little hand. "I am used to taking care of predicaments without the help of soldiers."

With those words, she gave a great sigh and put her head on my shoulder.

chapter 23

Birdie

I could see quite a bit through the bars of the door as Nicholas used his tractor to smash his way with my crate through the brush and down the tangly path. We passed Bajo's shanty and giant heaps of rusted sugarcane machinery. I knew where we were headed, but I didn't want to believe it. And then we were there, the tractor stopping at the concealed edge of the stone well, my crate suspended over space.

I heard Nicholas grunt as he shoved at the crate from behind.

"Roll up, Bugs," he cried out, suddenly protective again. "You're going to crash!"

We smashed down inside the shaft, the crate jamming at a slight angle before it could fall any distance. I was thrown against its wall, my shoulder painfully bruised.

Morgan groaned.

"Damn it, Nicholas!" I yelled. "That *hurt*!"

I thought I heard him laugh. If I'd had room I'd have kicked something.

A few inches of morning light shone through the top of the barred door. And here came the helicopters! I heard them, and so did Nicholas.

He quickly pulled the tarp over us, cutting off the little light we had. It was instantly breathless inside. I heard a few scoops of dirt being tossed on top, then the sound of branches and leaves being dragged over, placed overhead. The well had been nearly invisible when I'd first come upon it: Our crate would never be seen.

The tractor pulled back and the engine was cut. Parked, I imagined, inside the metal equipment building.

Nicholas would be running back to meet the coast guard, his smile and handshake ready. There was nothing else he could do. The island was too small for him to hide. He couldn't outrun them or shoot them all—and we had the only hiding place.

He'd try to talk his way out of it. But all the charm and money in the world wasn't going to get him out of this one. They'd find him, and they'd make him show them where we were hidden, and then we'd get rescued.

I was trapped inside a very small, dark, hot place, but thanks to the boat, I'd had practice doing what I had to do now: stay calm and keep my thoughts positive.

I could do that.

I smiled. Kirin would be proud of my Positive Thinking. Except I actually *was* a positive thinker. Kirin never had been. Not before, during, or after Nu-Way. I felt sad for the things she'd been through, but none of them were anything like being kidnapped by a maniac who stole boats and people and maybe even . . . well, did unspeakable harm to them. It occurred to me that Kirin had been born with a bad attitude.

I wondered how we'd been friends as long as we had.

o o o

Not only was it hot down here, it smelled very bad. I drew shallow breaths, tried to think about good things. I decided to make up a list in my mind. If I redid my room back in Riverton, what color would I make it? I imagined sheer curtains, a fluffy new comforter, a thick, cheerful rug. It was a contest for myself, remembering each item in the right order. In the end I could see the whole room transformed from blues and purples and greens into yellows and pinks and oranges. Built-in sunshine for long winter days.

I sat on the bench. Morgan was still on the floor, under my bare feet. My toes were snuggled into the crick of her elbow. I hoped she didn't mind, but it was very comforting.

I regretted trying to push her out. Without her here, the sound of her slow breathing, I'd probably already be hysterical.

I intended to stay calm and be a good example. Morgan was no doubt going to freak out when she woke up.

I hoped she *would* wake up. Surely she wasn't going to die!

This had all happened to her because I lured her in with my light. It was clear enough she and Nicholas weren't the sweethearts I'd thought they were. Or why would she have been sneaking around?

I wished she'd wake up and tell me her story.

○ ○ ○

I'd felt the helicopters as much as I heard them. Once they'd landed, at least one of them was quickly back in the air, roaming back and forth, very low overhead, searching. The crate thrummed with the slow beat of rotors.

I was both confident that they would find us soon—Calista was so small!—and terrified that they wouldn't! What if Nicholas found a way to turn them away? He was so tricky, I'd never been able to guess what he was up to!

And if that happened, would he come back for us? Or leave us here to die?

My hand kept going back to my vest pocket, touching the inhaler for reassurance. So far, I was okay—as long as I could fly away inside my head, I sensed I'd be okay.

Nicholas was a truly confused person. Why would he give me my inhaler to keep me alive, and at the same time put me in a box where I could die? What kind of person did stuff like this?

The same kind that said *whatever,* when you told them they were crazy . . .

○ ○ ○

I'd never known anyone named Morgan. Actually, it sounded more like a boy's name. This girl wore her hair short enough to be a boy. *Was* she a boy? A shocking idea. Of course she wasn't; I'd seen her naked; she was as girly as it gets.

She could be gay, though. One of my friend's sisters was gay, and she'd changed her name from Judith to Jude, a sort of either-way name like Morgan. But what about the kissing on the beach? She was way into that kiss!

"Morgan? Can you wake up?" I gently waggled her shoulder.

I had to do this about sixty times, but she finally quivered and woke.

She was confused about the dark, where she was . . . who I was. I tried not to shock her; I mean she was in a box with a complete stranger. If she knew I'd been kidnapped, she'd know she had been too.

She called me Oona. I wondered if Oona was a friend she'd left back on her boat. I hoped not. Who knew where her boat was! It could be at the bottom of the sea, scuttled so no one would ask questions. I had no idea where Nicholas had taken the boats or what he'd done with Bajo. For all I knew, he'd cooked him!

The main thing, for the moment, was to try to reassure Morgan, let her get used to being inside a crate.

She was supercool about it, only once trying to leap up. She sat silently by my side, but I sensed how much was going on inside her. Her hands reached to pat every inch of the crate. She used her fingers to push and prod each crack; she checked inside the supply box; plucked at the plastic spoons.

She did by nature what I hadn't even thought of doing: exploring every possibility of escape. She was not going to just wait here for rescue!

It was pretty much up to me for conversation.

"Morgan, I was wondering, is Nicholas your boyfriend?"

"No."

"Well then, why'd you come back?"

"I had concerns. I knew the black boat belonged to an elderly couple."

Mueti and *Papi.* The names on the hand towels.

She said, "I came back to see if they were Nicholas's captives . . . but it is you who are."

I nodded in the dark, spoke without thinking. "And you."

"Yes."

"So—you were going to rescue them? How?"

"With my strength and cunning."

Hmmm.

I'd seen what happened, how easily Nicholas had just jumped out and hit her on the head. But I didn't see how sharing that would help anything.

"Aren't you kind of young to have your own boat? Where are your folks? Are you on vacation?" I paused but she didn't answer. "Um, I mean this in a complimentary way, but is English your second language?"

She carefully cleared her throat.

"I have five first languages. English is one of them."

I waited. She shifted, understanding that I expected more.

"My parents were from Norway." She stopped. "I am not."

Her answers came more and more hesitantly.

"I live on the sea." She tried again. "I . . . I . . ."

The desperation in her voice was terrible.

"It's okay. I'm way too nosy." I wretchedly fiddled with the thin length of scarf that was still wrapped around my waist. I was more than nosy. I was cruel to ask questions of a beat-up girl who'd awakened to complete weirdness. And I suspected that even on her best days, she wasn't big on conversation. "Who cares whether languages are first or second? The awesome thing is you have five of them. Not that you need to speak at all!" I knew I was babbling, but I couldn't seem to stop. "I have approximately one and a half languages. *Que tal, amiga, vaya con Dios.*"

She'd taken her pocketknife out—she carried a knife!—and was prying at the metal hinges and bars on the door. The door definitely was the ricketiest part, but since just beyond the door was a stone wall, I didn't see how it would help even if she got it loose.

"Bad wood," she murmured. "And the nails are too short." Then she said, in that formal way of hers, "Please describe our environment outside of the box."

I did, in more detail than I'd realized I knew.

She recounted, "We are wedged into a stone well surrounded by jungle." Her voice was thoughtful. "We are positioned near the well's surface. But since our wooden box is nearly level, we must be more or less the same diameter as the well."

I hadn't thought of that. I said, "So if the box was jolted hard, and it leveled out, we'd fall in."

"Mmm. If the box is actually smaller, yes. I suspect we can count on Nicholas to have intended for it to fall to the bottom."

I hadn't envisioned us just resting over space, but the idea of dropping deep into the earth, maybe breaking our necks when we landed, left me weak.

"And perhaps three feet above us," she continued, "is the

opening of the well, which is covered with a plastic sheet and debris?"

"That's about it."

She was wet with sweat. I popped a can of Aquarium for her.

"Distilled," she said after a long swallow. "Flat tasting, but safe. . . . May I see the flashlight for a moment? I understand we need to be careful with the batteries."

She inspected everything again and then brought the light to rest on my face.

"Forgive me," she said, and snapped off the flashlight. "I'm rude to put the light in your eyes."

"Is your middle name Penelope?"

"No."

She stepped up on the bank of cans and bent double, pressing upward with her back. The boards groaned and dirt showered between the door and the stone wall. She pushed harder. She was unbelievably strong. Suddenly the crate shifted, alarming both of us.

She said, "Do you estimate this well is deep? That we could fall a distance if we were dislodged?"

"Yes. Both those things. Don't make us fall, okay?"

"And nothing around us but natural jungle? How does it happen that a well was built here?"

"Oh. I guess I forgot to mention a few things. The well's in the middle of an old ruin. There's all kinds of rusted metal machinery out there, giant wheels and copper tanks for making sugar. Bajo's hut's here. There's a garage for the tractor and stuff."

"Mmm."

I imagined her thoughts building around us in the dark: solid geometrical shapes that fit tightly one against the other. Stepping-stones that would lead us out of here.

"And that odor," she asked. "What is it?"

"I don't have a clue. Dead mice?"

I listened to her swallow water in the dark. Every minute since she'd wakened, I'd been more in awe of her. She was scary strong, and completely in charge of herself. Maybe of me as well! This was somehow more reassuring than frightening.

After a silence, which she seemed to prefer over talk, she said, "You are not Oona."

"No. I'm sorry. I'm Birdie Sidwell."

"Of course you're not Oona. I knew it could not be."

"No. I'm just Birdie, short for Birdwinkle, but don't tell anyone."

I wanted to add that I too was an amazing person, but I decided to be like she was and leave the world to figure that out.

"Are you named in honor of Bivens Birdwinkle?" she asked. "Without his brilliant discovery of certain properties of beans—"

"*You've heard of Bivens Birdwinkle?*" Even my science teacher never had! Morgan was beyond amazing!

"I would like to know how you come to be here, Birdwinkle."

She spoke *Birdwinkle* with such respect, I almost didn't mind it being my name.

It took about two hours to explain how I'd gotten here. In the end, I'd filled her in on Riverton and our special plans for this year and what happened at the dock and everything I knew about Nicholas.

She didn't say a word until I finished. And then she still said nothing.

"I can write," I added. "And tell stories . . . if it comes to that."

She made a soft sound that I think was laughing.

There had been no more helicopter sounds after the crate was covered over. I imagined that the men were now searching the island on foot. It could take a while to find us. It was cooking-hot, but if we could handle the dark, we could handle the heat.

○ ○ ○

Morgan turned out to be an expert at peeing in a bucket and then disposing of it. The whole routine was way complicated because of how crowded we were, but she made it seem matter-of-fact. I copied her exactly.

We were quiet for a while and then I said, "Is that your Le Cosmétique in Nicholas's art room?"

I really doubted she owned a large pink makeup case, but I had to ask.

"No."

"Do you think it's possible he's brought other girls here, you know, stolen them . . . or hurt them?"

225

She paused. "Yes."

"Do you think the reason he's so good at tricking people is because he's handsome?"

I took her silence to mean she was thinking about it.

"He is quite fine-looking. . . . I was . . . influenced . . . when I met him first. He had a beard then . . . blond hair."

"He was blond when I met him too! No beard, but there was a big scar—"

"I remember now. It was on his neck—"

"On his cheek, for St. Maarten. It's fake, a really horrible rubber thing." I didn't like remembering. It brought too close to mind my last glimpse of Mom and Dad.

A moment later I said, "The way he looks now? Dark hair, blue eyes, serious eyebrows? That's his real self, he's told me that. I believe him, I guess . . . even though I know he lies. He's very bad."

"Yes."

We were silent for a moment. Then I added, "The worst."

She laughed softly. "Oh, Birdie. I am unused to you."

"But you're getting used to me?"

"Yes, I believe I am."

I could feel her smiling. I was smiling too.

o o o

As the day passed, Morgan hesitantly told me her story. Not that she was much on details, but even the basics were enough if you'd had a life like she had! It was both the saddest and the most exciting life I'd ever heard of!

"What your folks need is a rehab program. They'd have one even in Panama. I mean that's where the *canal* is, that was an American deal; they must have left *programs* behind. Support groups, AA, that kind of thing?"

"I am unaware of this."

"So were you thinking you'd just never see them again? They'd do their thing, you'd go off and do yours?"

"I was thinking that."

"That's really heavy, Morgan. I mean I still *sleep* with my parents sometimes. I mean I *ask* to, they mostly don't let me, just Sunday mornings . . ."

She did that little thing she does.

"Morgan? . . . Just then, when you whispered *Oona?* Is that like a comfort to you?" The next thing I said was hard. Embarrassing. "I call for my mommy sometimes, since I've been here . . . when I get scared."

She didn't say anything.

After a while, I snapped open a can of pineapple. We sucked the sweet circles dry, then nibbled them, passing the time.

"Yes," Morgan said. "I call Oona when I am scared. Also."

"It helps, just saying the name."

"It isn't just saying the name." After another pause she said, "She comes to me with answers. This is perhaps a delusion, I see it now."

"Oh no, she's your imaginary hero is all. I've been doing the same thing with my friend back home. Kirin. She's only partly as heroic as I pretend, but the idea of her makes me brave. See? You imagine someone, and they give you the answers—"

"Yes," she whispered.

"Only it's you all the time!" It was actually only as I spoke that I realized this was true. If I were home with Kirin this very minute, she'd be disappointing me. "So," I went on, feeling proud at figuring this out, "you're the one who makes them up and you're the one who knows the answers!"

I knew I was babbling again, but I was getting a little anxious. I sensed the setting of the sun, in the way you can even if you're in a windowless place. It had been too long! We should have been discovered. A kind of despair settled in.

Morgan felt my body sag, reached to hold my hand.

chapter

24

morgan

I felt as much in peril within myself as without. More
so, as I was used to ordinary risk and danger. It was
my heart that was unused to invasion.

Birdie was not yet an adult, I was much more a grown person, and yet she knew things I did not. Her own heart was a sure
place, open to the world, unflinching.

I found myself yielding to the unfamiliar flow of intimacy.

"Aren't you lonely," she'd said, "without friends?"

I nodded. "I am searching for my own kind. I would like to
find friends, others who live at sea on their own, and are young
and have lost their families."

"Well, what are the chances of *that*?" she said. "I mean, I
never heard of anyone like you! And if you found someone just
like you, you'd both just sail away in different directions!"

She handed me three tiny chocolate pills, feeding me like I
was a baby cockatoo . . . or was this the way among friends?

She said, "Think what it is you like in people—with me the
number one thing is *kindness*. If I think someone's going to be
mean behind my back—like my best friend, Kirin, is—it kills

me. It's why it didn't really work out for us. Even though I still call her my best friend, and we want to be, we're not."

Birdie's best friend sounded like many people I'd observed.

"M&M?" She handed me another chocolate. "And then think about what you can give back, I mean for you that's *lots*. You know everything about how things work—"

I had just explained to her the mechanism of extracting juice from cane and synthesizing it into sugar.

"And I can tell you can kick butt—let me feel your biceps—*damn!* Anyone would want you for a friend!"

She made the world sound a simple place, as though constant exchanges of the heart and mind were normal, and available to anyone.

I put another of the candies on my tongue, felt my teeth gently shatter the shell, the inside suddenly exposed and melting. Was this what was happening to me? Was I being transformed by the friendship of this strange child?

If I melted, and Oona was inside me, would she not be lost as well?

And what of my parents? Was it true there was another way for them? My head ached inside and out. I saw that friendship was irksome as well as gladdening.

I turned to silence. For a long while, my mind worked on the possibilities of escape.

I said, "Approximately how far are we from my boat?"

"It's gone, Morgan. Nicholas took it away somewhere; he was gone a long time. And Bajo, his worker, took the black boat, but he never came back. Nothing's left but a little fishing boat in a building near here, and the motorboat at the dock—"

I no longer heard her words. The *Svanhild* was gone! Birdie could never understand the effect of her words. My sailboat was my world. I had no Riverton to go to, no family waiting for my return. By coming to stop Nicholas I had lost everything!

Oona?

Oona?

Had even my sister left me?

Was I now utterly alone?

O O O

Night fell. I knew it with certainty. I had been patient with Birdie's hopes for rescue, and with her fears of endangerment. But no one would find us here. I knew that with certainty as well.

But how to tell her it was time to act, without terrifying her? She had a respiratory illness she dreaded would return.

"Birdie, I believe you are able to stay calm at will. You advised me to breathe deeply when I woke. Now you must breathe deeply. I'm going to begin kicking the top off our enclosure." I took her hand. "If we fall, we will then deal with having fallen."

"Morgan! Don't! You'll knock the crate loose, we'll get killed!"

"Stop speaking." The crate groaned as I plopped her firmly on the floor. "Breathe deeply."

I positioned myself on my back on the bench. I heard Birdie there beside me in the dark, breathing fully and deliberately. I cocked my knees back to my chest—but before I could kick, I suddenly heard a splintering noise . . . followed by a small gasp. That quickly, the floor gave way under Birdie and she was gone. Her little voice trailed questioningly into space below, then a small, dull bump.

"Birdie?" I called. "Birdie! You must answer!"

What had I been thinking? To decide for both of us that falling was acceptable?

I did not cause the floor to break apart, but I went ahead without listening to her protests!

The crate *would* have fallen apart at my first kick, that was clear enough now!

For a moment, without light, I hesitated to move. I felt alongside the water-can bench. Next to it was ten inches of wooden flooring . . . then two feet of open space. Beyond, the floor resumed for the rest of the short distance to the wall. Not such a big hole. Just wide enough for Birdie's slight frame to slip through.

"Birdie! Answer!"

The silence opened, ate my words.

I had climbed stone walls before, in play. In abandoned plantations just such as this, on other sugar-growing islands. I had done it many times, frolicked up and down like a monkey. The coral bricks could cause lasting sores from their scratches, but I have had far worse things.

I made a picture in my mind of the floor of the crate (manageable), of the stone walls (slick), of the well's bottom (wet). I did not believe the shaft was filled with water. I'd heard no splash. The great mystery would be how far down my friend lay, and how serious her injuries.

If she remained unconscious, I would wait below with her, wait for help to come, until the morning. Protect her from rats and spiders. If help did not come, I would climb back up, kick my way through the crate, and find ropes to bring her up. A simple plan.

I began.

The greatest danger was getting myself positioned for the descent. If more planks were to give, I too would fall. I must hold firmly on to the crate until I achieved footholds in the stone cracks, then transfer my hands one at a time to the wall. A job best done slowly and heedfully.

I squatted on the lip just next to the can bench and felt the gap in the middle of the floor. The missing boards were still attached by their nails, swinging down alongside the wall. I hoped they would remain attached. They would be a nasty thing to fall on poor Birdie.

I extended a leg through the hole, angling it until I felt the wall with my bare toes. I was suddenly glad of their length and agility. I found lovely large square-cut blocks of coral randomly set between stone and conventional brick. Gaping spaces everywhere!

I grasped the edge of a floorboard on either side of me and lowered myself. Reaching as far down as I could with my feet, I chinked my toes into fat cracks. Then I lunged my upper body toward the wall, transferred one handhold to the wall; another. The wall was not even slimy, at least not the porous coral blocks. As long as I went slowly, it would be easy.

"Birdie?"

Nothing. Nothing beyond heat and a dismal odor and a sense that the well breathed in and out of its own accord. If only I had Birdie's flashlight, I would know so much more! But it was in her vest pocket. I wouldn't know I was there until I was there. My wounded head was a distraction.

And then my foot slipped on the edge of a coral, my own blood slickening the stone.

As I descended, water began to seep around me. The edges of stone became round with moss and fungi. My cut foot had begun to throb, so I took my mind elsewhere.

Oona? Oona, I'm saving my friend.

Have you left me, Oona, because I have a friend?

Will you not even say goodbye?

The familiar voice came at last . . . though I could barely hear it.

Listen to yourself . . . only.

As her words trailed away, I recognized the voice as mine.

No! I could not exist without her.

My toe grip suddenly failed me. I dangled by my fingers, cutting them deeply as I scrambled with my feet for another crack—

There was no point in calling Oona for help. Oona was . . . dead.

o o o

I struggled frantically, experiencing, as if for the first time, the complete burden of my weight.

It seemed like forever, my arms racked with pain, and then one foot found a jagged crack off to one side. I pushed roughly into it, clung in place, waited for my heart to calm.

Around me, the well rasped in mock respiration.

Only it was not the well! It was Birdie, her labored breath suddenly loud in my ears. She was alive and she was having an asthma attack!

"Birdie, I'm coming for you!"

"Uh." A short gasp, much closer than I'd thought.

The next step down I found myself knee-deep in . . . something! I had reached the bottom!

"Birdie, I am here."

Her inhalations were slow and appalling.

I felt across the mounded surface of the floor: It was alternately moth-smooth and slimy. Her body was arched there, rigid with the effort of taking in oxygen. She was deeply embedded in *stuff*, its suffocating earth-mold smell leaking from where she'd broken its surface. The heavy stink of death lurked beneath.

Her vest pockets were empty, the contents spilled in the fall. I dug through pillows of the brittle fleshlike stuff, and suddenly my hand was around the flashlight . . . the inhaler right alongside!

I gave it a small shake: so little remained!

I felt for Birdie's head, lifted it, and brought the inhaler to her mouth. She grabbed at it and depressed the tube, shuddering to get its vapor into her lungs.

I flicked on the flashlight. Its dim beam glanced off the wet stone walls. I brought it to Birdie's face: The skin around her eyes and her mouth was bluish. She strained with the task of keeping herself alive.

Spread deep around us was a kingdom of mushrooms. A giant billow of mushrooms filled the well's bottom, mushroom caps an arm's length across.

This made no sense to me—mushrooms cannot grow on rock. They must have nutrients, an organic host.

Birdie lay in their midst like Alice fallen into Wonderland. Her red curls spread over their broken flutes, her slender little legs curled inside her long skirt; she was covered with spores.

I held the little flashlight between my teeth and began examining her. I started at her head and felt carefully along her neck, her shoulders, her arms and legs. Each of my movements separated the edges of the mushroom caps and brought up puffs of mushroom dust.

None of Birdie's bones felt fractured or at an odd angle—but anything could have been hurt inside her.

I clicked off the light. "Do you feel any pain?"

"Uh-uh."

We sat there in the dark, Birdie propped up against me, waiting for the attack to pass.

"Mold," she whispered.

"Mmm. Fungi."

"Allergic," she said, and returned her attention to careful breathing.

I snapped the flashlight back on. Why did mushrooms grow here at all? I dug under the folds with my fingers and hit a hard slimy surface. I cleared a few inches: moldering wood. Using my forearm, I swept a broad path. Another crate! Very like ours. Crude lettering was spray-painted across it—

Birdie was leaned on her side, watching.

I read aloud, "V-u-n—"

"*Vunderweer!*" she cried. "It's *him* inside, *dead!* That's why it *stinks* in here—it's his *grave!*"

"Hush, Birdie, you need to calm yourself."

She was right, of course. This explained the lusty mushrooms—the damp wood, the nutrients within the corpse.

The owner of the island had been placed in a box like ours, thrown in the well as we were, and had perished—as we were expected to do.

We had to get out of here!

The excitement had quickened Birdie's breathing. I felt her pulse. Fast, but no faster than mine.

I turned off the flashlight. "We're going to climb back up now. You can't remain here breathing mushroom spores. I believe the inhaler is nearly finished."

"It is." She pressed close to me. "I fell right out of the crate, Morgan!"

"I am truly sorry."

"It wasn't your fault, it happened so fast—"

"Yes, but it could have been my fault; in a minute my kicks would have caused it."

"It's okay, really. . . . it's just weird—I was so afraid this would happen, I didn't want to take a chance at escaping and then it happened anyway. . . . Thank you for saving me."

She reached to hug me, and I hugged her back. Such a small person, hardly bigger than Lita, my young Venezuelan friend—

She jerked back. "Did you say climb up the wall? Were you thinking I could climb up there? No way, I *can't*—"

"Breathe deeply."

"I am breathing deeply." She was. "But I can't climb up there."

"You can. You just need for me to show you how. Stand up now."

I untied the long fabric of her skirt, then faced her away from me and tied us both together with it. "Don't think about danger, think about doing what you must do."

We would climb as one, Birdie positioned inside my own arms and legs. No great weight would hang from me in that way. Even I could not climb out with her full weight. If she slipped, she would have the safety of being tied—if I could hold us both in place . . .

My job was to stay braced as she went up a step at a time. Her job was to make sure each step was done carefully.

I showed her.

She was shaking her head, but when I nudged her with my knee, she stepped up onto the wall.

"*Ow!*" she said. "That hurts my feet . . . *and* my hands. . . . How many times do I have to do this before we're there?"

"Very many."

We went up a few feet, and then I felt her tense up again, her breathing become jagged. She was very afraid.

I said, "It is all right to speak . . . tell me about the fall, and begin moving upward."

She nodded against my chest. "I don't remember the fall, or crashing." I nudged her and she lifted a leg, brought herself up a notch. "I think it was just the shock or something, but I was knocked out for a minute. When I woke up, I thought it was Sunday—that it was Sunday morning, and I was at home, in Riverton, in my parents' bed."

She was moving nicely upward.

"They have a pillow-top mattress, that really nice kind? And a feather bed thing on top of that? It's like the best bed in the world, at least that I've ever been in. I wish I could sleep in it every night right there between them, but of course I *can't*, except Sunday morning I get to . . ."

In this way we climbed steadily to the crate.

". . . and the best Sundays of all are when Dad brings up fresh-squeezed orange juice—we get crates of them shipped from Florida every December—and—"

"We are there, Birdie."

"At the crate? No way! I climbed the whole well! I am so awesome!"

She was definitely feeling better.

I said, "The next part is a little tricky."

"Trickier than *climbing*?"

"No more, no less, just take one thing at a time."

I was untying the fabric around our waists.

"No-no-no! Don't undo me from you, Morgan! I mean it!"

"Here, I'm tying it back on you. You don't have to do anything until I'm back in the crate. Then I'll reach down and you'll hand me the end of the fabric. I'll swing you up. That's all we have to do."

Her body had gone rigid again.

"Breathe, hold on. When I'm back in the crate, I'll tell you exactly what to do."

I reached for the floorboard, grabbed tight with both hands, tucked my knees up, and snapped my legs up through the crack. I quickly stood on the remaining boards . . . and took a great breath.

"Are you all right, Birdie?"

"Yes."

There was no way she could get in the way I had. She didn't have the strength or the skill. I lay facedown on the floor and stretched my arm toward her.

"Give me the end of the fabric now. One hand is plenty to keep you in place."

It took a minute and then her damp little hand briefly pushed inside mine, passing me a wad of thin cloth.

"Relax now, Birdie. Do nothing to hold yourself in place, do not jump, do not struggle. I'm going to swing you in with the cloth. We need to do this quickly but smoothly. Imagine it."

"I'm imagining."

"Get ready."

I gritted my teeth and dug my toes in. She must come up with the first pull—if she was left dead weight dangling from the cloth, I would never get her in.

"Come *now*."

Her weight hit the end of the cloth, and I swung her up. She was grabbing for the edge of the crack, and I had her. I rolled over on my back, pulling her on top of me.

"Whoa!" she said. "Don't ask me to do that again."

I didn't plan to. My heart banged inside my chest. It was not at all the same, saving others, as it was saving yourself!

I said, "Stand up now, and step over the crack to the bench. We need to distribute our weight. I'll tie your cloth to the door in case the floor gives way again."

"And then I should climb up the door and kick my way out?"

"Yes, but only if the crate already starts to give. It's very fragile now." My head throbbed. I'd had many injuries in my life, but none had left me feeling such need to sleep. "I must rest for just a few minutes; then I will take it apart bit by bit."

"Okay."

"It is dangerous, being here."

"Yes," Birdie said. "I've been trying to tell you."

chapter 25

Birdie

It was a funny thing, lying there on top of my sleep-ing bag, on top of the bank of water cans. My hands and feet were like *ruined* from the climb, and my knees were beat up, everything on me hurt, and I'd had the worst asthma at-tack of my entire life, including the first one brought on by the flying pot of geraniums. I was in the dark, in a kind of under-ground coffin, with a dead man below somewhere, growing mushrooms out of him. And the coast guard was taking its time about rescuing me. But instead of feeling freaked out, I felt re-laxed and . . . *brave*.

"Think it's still night, Morgan?"

Her voice was weary. "I estimate it is between midnight and three A.M."

"So we should go to sleep?"

"For a few minutes. Yes."

I was beginning to think she never got tired, or hurt, or even hungry.

I knew I wouldn't sleep. I'd never been so excited.

I fell asleep immediately and dreamed about the Ducks. We were doing drills, and my shots one after the other whizzed past Meredith, our excellent goalie. I was cranking up the points.

"*Look at her go*," the girls were all saying.

My feet were like thunder-feet, bang-banging the ball across the gym in short powerful bursts—bam . . . bam . . . *bam*—

My eyes flew open. The sound was real! The walloping came from right on top of the crate!

"Stay calm, girls!" came a muffled voice. "Lie down on the floor and don't move!"

The coast guard was here! A sound of joy gurgled out of me. I did as I was told and remained lying down. Morgan did not do as she was told. She sprang to her feet and crouched next to me. The tenseness of her body radiated inside the crate.

"Lie down, Morgan," I said. "Be still like they told us."

She was so catlike, I actually thought I heard her growl.

"I slept," she said. "I'm sorry. We should have escaped."

"It's okay! We're being rescued!"

That growl again, and then the tarp was flapped to the side. Dusty shafts of dawn's light shone through the crack at the top of the door.

They were here!

"Don't move, Birdie," Morgan whispered. "Leave this to me!"

In the murky light, I could just barely make her out, poised with a foot on either side of the crack. Her profile was still new to me.

"I said *lie down!*" came the voice again. I heard a note of panic in it. "I'm coming inside!"

"You can't!" I said. "There's no room and our crate's falling apart! Don't you mean you want us to come *out?*"

The top was being violently ripped off.

"Shut up and move over, Bugs. Don't make me cut your sweet little throat."

Nicholas! Looming over us, gripping Bajo's machete. He glanced anxiously over his shoulder. "*Move it!* This is *my* hidey-hole—why do you think I put food in here, girls? For *you?*" He lowered a leg down, poked Morgan's shoulder with the machete. "Go for your knife and I'll slice your arm off."

She sprang straight up, knocking him backward, toppling him back onto land. She was immediately out of the crate, and on him.

"Climb up here, Birdie!" she yelled. "Hide in the jungle!"

The machete clattered past me and down the well. She'd already gotten his weapon away from him!

*Oof*ing animal noises told me they were wrestling each other.

I scrambled through the opening and was half-blinded by sunlight. I knelt carefully on top of the remains of the teetering, creaking, crumbling crate and peeked over the lip of the well.

They were rolling around between pieces of broken sugar-cane machinery, tumbling back to wedge against the stone edge of the well. They held each other as tightly as they had that night on the beach. Morgan's jaw was clenched with effort but her eyes were calm. She looked directly into Nicholas's face.

His teeth were hideously bared, ready to eat her alive. He was so much bigger than she was! His shapely arms bulged with muscle.

She freed one hand long enough to grab at his face. He flinched as she tore off an eyebrow! The thick black *fake* caterpillar-thing fell into the ferns.

I blinked at his face, not two yards away from me. One eye scowled fiercely, the other was blankly expressionless. I reached down through the crate's roof, grabbing for any sort of weapon. I jerked out a whole six-pack of Aquarium, the motion fatally jarring the crate. I felt it give under my feet and scuttled onto land just as it cracked apart, fell piece by piece into the well.

"*Birdwinkle . . .*" It was Morgan. I could barely hear her over a crash that seemed to go on forever.

Nicholas was sitting on her, arms braced as he dug his thumbs into her neck, strangling her. She flailed under him, her face losing all color.

I flew ten years back in time and landed in the Kimballs' backyard. Only this time, I wasn't the one in the sandbox. I was the hurler of missiles. I heaved the six-pack like it was a pot of geraniums—only my aim was perfect! The clanking cans twisted through the air and hit Nicholas right on his pretty face. His head snapped back, and Morgan leaped free.

He staggered to rise. She kicked him in the chest. He grabbed for her arm and she elbowed him in the neck, then was behind him, clobbering him over the head with a rusted hunk of metal. He lay there looking dead.

She broke off a length of vine, yanked his arms behind him,

roughly tied him up. The bald eye was leaned into the brush, as though he were trying to hide it.

A man's voice boomed into the morning. "Step back! Step back! Get him—"

A dozen strong, uniformed bodies surrounded us, heads swiveling to take in the situation.

The man with the deep voice was the leader. A handsome young man with a no-nonsense face. His features reminded me of the Claknee tribesmen in Oregon.

He nodded at Morgan as if he knew she was the one who'd saved us. I thought he'd at least compliment her, I mean it was pretty amazing what she'd done. But like Morgan, he wasn't one to waste words. He told his squad to check Nicholas for weapons, get cuffs on him.

He was very much in charge. I suddenly became aware that every part of my body hurt. My legs trembled as I stepped forward, hand out.

I meant to shake his hand and say, *I'm Birdie Sidwell, the kidnapping victim. This is my best friend, Morgan. She saved me from death. Then I saved her.*

I meant to say a lot of things, but my voice had gone very small. "Where's my mom?"

He took my hand in his. "We'll get her on the radio soon as we get you back to the house."

His words were slow, but his grab for me was quick. I realized my knees had buckled and it was only his sudden arm around my waist that kept me from sliding to the ground.

I leaned against him, stared dazedly over at Morgan. She'd

gone very quiet. I glanced at the bruises on her neck. Could she still talk after being choked like that? As if she could read my mind, she gave her head a tiny bow, meaning she was all right.

I nodded and roused myself, moved to stand on my own. "We're both fine, Admiral."

"Chief," he corrected me in an earnest voice. "Chief Brightwater. United States Coast Guard."

A soldier wrapped a blanket around my shoulders, gave me a carton of orange juice to sip.

Morgan stood gazing at the chief's dusky, broad-featured face as if trying to decide if he was her rescuer or her captor.

"Miss?" he spoke directly to her. "You have no reason to fear me—I mean the coast guard."

He certainly didn't know Morgan. She wasn't afraid of anything. . . . Or was she?

"Did this man kidnap you? Both of you?" He held out a crumpled police sketch, captioned *Wesley Nicholas*. The three of us stared at it. Nicholas's eyes had been penciled in a dark color, but otherwise were the same: large, luminous, innocent-looking. I knew Mom had noticed them. My parents had also remembered the pale, nearly invisible brows, the blond hair and scar.

"I'm not sure this is Wesley Nicholas," the chief said, bending over Nicholas's half-hidden face.

"Pull on his eyebrow," I said. "It comes off." No way was I going to touch it. Everything about Nicholas disgusted me.

Chief Brightwater tugged it and it came away with his fingers.

Wesley Nicholas's face was now facing fully upward. Gruesomely bald. Unfamiliar. He groaned and opened blank eyes.

I wanted to say, *You said you were showing me the real you. But there is no real you!*

I knew I was talking to myself.

Chief Brightwater stood, the black eyebrow stuck to his outstretched finger like a fuzzy leech. "The scar was fake too?"

I nodded.

"Get him back to the chopper."

Two soldiers carried Nicholas off.

"Let's get you both to the medic, get your parents on the radio."

Morgan glanced at me, eyes apprehensive. She *was* afraid of the coast guard! I remembered she was a runaway, still too young to legally be on her own.

I mouthed *Don't worry* to her. She nodded very solemnly and looked relieved.

The soldiers took our arms, headed us to the Jeep. I was exhausted, but there was still so much the chief needed to know. "Look down at the bottom of the well." My voice had slowed to a crawl. "Under all the boards? We think it's Peter Vunderweer in there. Dead."

Chief Brightwater's face tightened. "We'll get the debris out. We knew he was missing. You're both very lucky."

"Is there a girl missing too? Maybe named Penelope?"

"There are missing girls." He squinted sadly at the horizon, as if he were in charge of finding all the missing girls of the world.

Someone started up the Jeep.

"You need to rest now."

As we headed out of the jungle and down the knoll to the house, we heard a helicopter thrum to life. It was parked down on the beach, its orange-and-white colors cheerful in the morning light. Two burly men in uniforms pushed Nicholas—*Wesley Nicholas*—in front of them. He was fully conscious now and looked both completely the same and entirely changed. Without his eyebrows, he had the smooth, bland face of a baby. His hands were cuffed in front of him.

Just before he climbed the steps up to the helicopter's hatch, he turned toward us. The force of the rotors lifted his dark hair and showed the bruise where the cans had hit him. He looked straight at the Jeep.

"G'dye, mates," he called. "Or is it g'bye? G'bye, my princesses, one and all."

His smile was brilliant, the Australian accent perfect.

The guard pulled on his arm, but Nicholas stood there another moment, squinting against the sun to see me.

"Bugs? One last thing—what's my story's real ending? The surprise?"

His story? It was *my* story! The things he'd stolen from me galloped across my mind like frenzied ponies—my family, my health, my own *thoughts*!

The power in my voice surprised us all. "You walk the plank, Nicholas!"

His eyes closed for a moment. Then he pressed his shapely lips to the tropical air and tenderly blew us his kiss.

Morgan and I reached for each other's hand.

○ ○ ○

The house was in shambles. Nicholas had bashed apart his computers, cut phone lines, burned his papers in a frantic attempt to erase his deeds. He must have thought to the end that he would escape.

The coast guard had found his laptop and plugged it into a printer. Page after page of evidence cranked out.

A medic swabbed antiseptic on the cuts on our legs and arms, hands and feet. It hurt, but Morgan didn't make a whimper, so neither did I.

He felt carefully around the wound on Morgan's head.

"I believe you have a concussion."

She gave a tiny nod.

He looked into my eyes, listened to my chest.

"A little bronchitis?"

I shook my head. "Asthma."

"Doesn't sound bad."

I nodded.

Then the soldiers were smiling and I was being handed a heavy sort of walkie-talkie. "Press this button to talk. Someone's real anxious to say hi—"

"Mommy?"

"Birdie? Sweetheart?"

The connection, thin and delicate as a rainbow, arced over water, land, time, and brought our unbearable separation to an end.

Daddy's voice cut in, crackling with distance and emotion.

"Don't cry, honey, don't cry, we're in Florida; they'll bring you here tomorrow. . . . It's all over, honey."

Yes, I was nodding, tears streaming down my face. It was over.

Then the phone was gently lifted away and I was being picked up, carried into the guest room, tucked into bed. The last words I heard were Morgan speaking to Chief Brightwater:

"No—my parents cannot be reached at this time."

I knew she meant that in a more important sense than anyone would guess. Then I was in the deepest sleep of my life.

o o o

I woke slowly, images swimming through my head: Mom in her silver-blue Volvo, picking me up from school exactly on time; Dad pinching back tomato plants, the pollen smell exhilarating; my girlfriends dressing in freshly laundered soccer uniforms. The cool misty streets of Riverton just before dark.

Beyond the hum of Peter Vunderweer's guest room fan was the low murmur of male voices, the soft thump of batches of papers being aligned.

Where was Morgan? Had she slept in Nicholas's room?

The shutters in my room had been closed, but brilliant light burst through every crack. I'd be seeing my parents today! Meeting them at a hospital in Miami for every kind of checkup.

I stretched my sore arms and legs. Nothing broken. Nothing but a few bruises and cuts on a small body that was 100% alive.

The room was hot despite the fan. The sheets were sweaty,

and I was still dressed in clothes I'd worn for several days. I straggled into the guest room shower and afterward dressed in my best slacks and long-sleeved T-shirt. I didn't want Mom and Dad to see the nasty coral cuts up and down my shins and forearms. Not first thing. They'd been through enough.

I was feeling happy and excited by the time I went into the kitchen and greeted everyone. Several soldiers jumped up from the table to greet me. Chief Brightwater handed me a mug of coffee just like I was one of his men.

"May I have some toast, too?" I glanced at the cupboard where the bread was kept, then at the toaster. "Evenly done and not too much butter?"

He rose with a confused expression, took a few steps toward the cupboard, then recovered, nodded to a grinning soldier to get on it.

"Not too much butter," the chief said sternly.

Morgan sat at the table, her back very straight. Her auburn eyes studied me in the same intense way in which she'd listened to me in the well.

I scooted my chair as close to hers as I could. She smiled at me, which for reasons I didn't understand, made me feel like bursting into tears.

Notebooks, two-way radios, field equipment were piled on the table. Soldiers milled around the house, outside, everywhere. They each wore the look of having an important job.

Down on the beach was a new assortment of helicopters. One said K-TV. Soldiers encircled several photographers and their video equipment like a human corral. A wild excitement abruptly replaced my tearfulness.

The chief's words were for me, but he was looking at Morgan.

"I have a few questions for you, Birdie. And you probably have a few for me."

"Yes, I do." I took a deep breath, trying to steady my emotions. "Who all got my e-mails? Was it Dad who sent you here? He's a bean genius, you know; his mind is very important to America."

Chief Brightwater opened his mouth, but I had more. "Why didn't you search the first time you came? I was in the black boat that Nicholas—Wesley Nicholas—took somewhere. Oh, and do you know about Bajo? Or where he is? Or where Morgan's boat is? It's named swan-something and it's very important to her."

The toast popped up. One of the soldiers made a snorting sound and then everyone was laughing. Even Chief Brightwater smiled and shook his head.

Everyone, here for me!

I don't know why, but if my hands and feet hadn't been so covered with Band-Aids, I would have jumped up and done a few cartwheels. I hadn't had that urge since Riverton, where the whole town was like this, one big friendly audience.

chapter
26

morgan

Buddy Brightwater—Chief Brightwater—and I stood on the dock at St. Maarten, next to a sign that said CHINGO'S FINE 3-TIME-A-DAY FERRY TO SANTE PETTS. Tied in front of us, restless in the trade winds, were two orphaned sisters, black and white: the *Engelberta* and the *Svanhild*. It was very fine, seeing my sailboat again. And a very eerie feeling, knowing this was the exact spot where Birdie had been stolen from her parents.

"There she is, Morgan."

It had taken five days, but he no longer called me miss.

"Thank you, Buddy."

Like me, he rarely smiled. I see now that this is a reflection of his earnest nature. He knows that everywhere there are people who require help, and he feels the need to help them.

We have talked of how we are alike in this way. We have talked of many things. Even of Oona. Buddy's people are Native American, from the Pacific Northwest. They have a different way of looking at things. He says there are mysteries in the world that do not require solving. I believe this to be so.

After Wesley Nicholas was taken away, I remained on Calista for several days, along with coast guard officers who collected evidence of his many crimes. Buddy was assigned as my liaison, a temporary custodian until my guardianship, citizenship, and legal right to the *Svanhild* were determined.

We do not yet know the fate of the German couple who owned the *Engelberta,* or the owners of the other stolen boats—many of which had been docked, and later sold from this slip. But there is reason to think that they have gone the way of Peter Vunderweer.

And there was more: false papers, the fencing of stolen goods, the laundering of bad money. Much more. Whatever opportunities came Nicholas's way—Wesley Nicholas's way—he took them.

Whatever young girl entertained him in some unique manner became his captive. If not on the island, then in other ways. The e-mails left on his computer told of many broken hearts, lucky girls who would never see his handsome face again.

The day after we were discovered, Birdie was flown to Miami, where her parents waited for her. They had haunted the coast guard headquarters, and in desperation, even called the president. Hope for her recovery had faded—until Birdie's e-mail arrived! Then Chief Brightwater took over, flying his specially trained men directly to Calista.

The family's perfect year was only perfect in that they regained their familyhood. Birdie called me yesterday on her new orange cellular phone. None of the Sidwells wanted to return to St. Maarten, or to go on with their plans at St. Petts.

Instead they are spending a week at Walt Disney World. Birdie says she's *always* wanted to go there and does not mind that reporters follow them wherever they go. She says answering questions and being on television and in the newspapers is just part of the price of being Birdie Sidwell. Her parents have made a deal with the media. They will cooperate now, but the reporters are not to follow them back to Riverton—a place Birdie describes as "the best place in the world." The reporters have left me alone. I am not "media friendly," they said. Which is fine with Buddy and me.

My own best place in the world remains the sea. It is my home. But when I return to it now, it will be for pleasure and not because of a fear of land, or the imagined shackles of land people. It was Birdie who taught me to say goodbye to old dreads and old griefs.

The greatest of those dreads, the law, is going easy on me. The *Svanhild* has been commandeered. Seized by the coast guard. This is not so harsh as it sounds. The boat and I must be returned to Panama and my parents, but Buddy has obtained permission for me to remain on board for the journey. He and Seaman Davis, a very nice boy just slightly older than I, will act as crew. I will reside in Panama until I am eighteen and a legal adult in that country.

I look forward to seeing my parents again. I hope to help them find a way out of their sad prison. Perhaps they will even remember, on the shortest day of the year, to carve my mark inside the belly of my boat.

Beyond that day, I have not foreseen.

What I know is that in a short time, Buddy and I have become friends. It is not a matter of time passing that determines friendship. It is for me, as it is for Birdie, a matter of recognizing the kindness of another's heart.

Christmas in Riverton is awesome. Red-and-green strings of lights are transformed by the winter mist into soft hazy loops of pink and teal, and the foghorns sound like something from nature.

It was just last summer that everything happened, but it seems more distant than that. I hardly remember why we were so big on leaving here. None of us, Mom or Dad or me, can remember. When the sun comes out, you can see clear across the river to the mountains of Washington. Riverton is the nicest small town in America. That's why Mom and Dad decided to raise me here in the first place.

Mom loves being back at work. Dad loves being back at his laptop. I really, really love being in the ninth grade. I'm a little taller. My nose is still small and straight. Coach Stinson let me start for our first Ducks game. Go, Ducks!

Of course now I'm like the hero of Riverton. I can't even walk to school without someone wanting to hear what happened in living detail.

I just say, "You can read all about it next spring, in my book."

Of course my being a nearly published authoress makes them think I'm even more awesome, so I usually stop and give them the highlights. Since I never have my umbrella, half the time I'm soaked before I get to school.

I don't care that much. There's more to Riverton than rain. The river, the streets, the houses are heaped with stories. I can hardly walk down the block without tripping over one.

I've changed my room around, filled it with bright color. Mom and Dad let me do it the way I'd planned in my head, and it came out great. For a while, I even had my pink-and-orange vest hanging on the wall, as decoration. But seeing it every morning when I woke up was too much. I packed it in my closet, along with the one picture I'd taken—my folks on the dock, innocently waving to me.

My therapist thought rewriting *The Adventures of Naughty Nicholas* would be a good way of dealing with whatever post-trauma syndrome might show up. Of course the story was never really about Wesley Nicholas anyway.

I put my heart into making it perfect. I included all the details that happened, plus some things that never happened. And I changed the heroine into a redheaded girl named Amy, sort of a combination of me and Morgan.

Amy's Awesome Adventures.

It was an exciting story, even to me. Mom sent it to Bright Lights, a publisher that specializes in young adults writing for other young adults. They knew my name from the kidnapping and wrote right back with an offer. I didn't even need an agent, although I have one now. A big one in Seattle.

When Mom and I go up to the city and "do lunch" with the agent, I also go see Kirin. She's still at Nu-Way, and of course she still hates it. Mom's done a lot to bring attention to the school, and it's not as bad as it used to be. At least so far Kirin hasn't been Nudelized.

I've tried to talk to her about what I went through, and how I understand what she's going through, but she doesn't really get it. She's more comfortable with me as a pocket pal than a real person. She's still a friend, but that moment of closeness we had before I left never came back again.

My true friend is Morgan. Friends forever. We e-mail each other. She has a boyfriend, that handsome coast guard chief. He's crazy about her. He was so much help when she first went back to Panama.

Her mom had gotten very sick. Morgan stayed on land with her, which was all she could do to make her feel better. In October, when I was busy opening presents and celebrating my fourteenth birthday, Morgan's mother died.

"I am sad," she wrote me. "Losing both my mother and my sister."

Another person would have gone on and on about their feelings—or like me, written a book. That isn't Morgan's way.

She also told me her dad quit drinking. He's decided to go back to Norway. I got my last e-mail from her a few days ago, December twenty-first, the shortest day of the year.

She wrote, "I am an adult now, by the law. Buddy has come today, to mark my birthday inside the *Svanhild*. Father has made her my own free boat. I will be sailing her to Puerto Rico soon. Buddy is stationed there. Your friend forever, Morgan."

It's a short e-mail, but it says a lot.

As far as post-traumatic stress syndrome goes, I really don't have it. I'm immune to stuff like that now. I don't even wheeze. I guess if I got dropped down another pit containing giant mushrooms and dead men, it could happen again. But mainly I'm not so fearful. I don't try so hard to keep up with others.

My parents blame themselves for everything. I've overheard them saying *It should never have happened.*

I'm not so sure.

Can't best things sometimes come from the worst? I survived being Nicholized and wrote the book I'd dreamed of writing.

And I met Morgan, who taught me how to climb out of the deep and into the light. Where everything is familiar, but not quite the same as before.

ABOUT THE AUTHOR

SUSANNA VANCE lives in a rainy village in Oregon, where stories sprout like mushrooms. Her first novel, *Sights,* originally a short story no bigger than a chanterelle, is an ALA Best Book for Young Adults. If you care to visit a world where cats and magic lurk in shadowed corners and teenagers leap about like divas of the rain forest, go to www.susannavance.com.